HEALING HEARTS

A SWEETGUM MEADOWS ROMANCE BOOK 13

IMANI PRICE

First Edition: November 2025

ISBN 979-8-89283-314-1 (ebook)
ISBN 979-8-89283-315-8 (paperback)

Published by Books to Hook Publishing, LLC.
www.BooksToHook.com

CONTENTS

Tasha Jenkins didn't know why she thought small-town medicine would be easier.

Standing in the cramped exam room of Sweetgum Meadows Family Clinic, she pressed her fingertips against her patient's wrist and counted the steady rhythm beneath weathered skin. Sixty-eight beats per minute. Normal. She released Earl Whitaker's arm and stepped back, pulling off her nitrile gloves with the practiced efficiency that had carried her through six years of emergency medicine in Atlanta.

The routine should have been comforting by now. Six months of treating minor cuts, checking blood pressure, and managing chronic conditions like diabetes and arthritis. Six months of knowing her patients' names, their families, their stories. It was everything she'd thought she wanted when she'd fled the chaos of Atlanta General's trauma bay.

So why did she still feel like she was holding her breath, waiting for the other shoe to drop?

"The infection's responding well to the antibiotics," she said, examining the healing cut that ran across the farmer's palm. The wound was clean, edges knitting together nicely, no signs of the angry red streaking that would indicate complications. "Keep it clean and dry, and come back if you see any redness or swelling."

Earl nodded, his calloused fingers already reaching for the worn baseball cap perched on the exam table. At seventy-two, he moved with the careful deliberation of someone who'd learned to respect his body's limitations, but his eyes were sharp and kind. "Appreciate it, Doc. That chainsaw got away from me something fierce."

"Chainsaws don't negotiate," Tasha said, making a note in his chart. Her handwriting was precise, each letter carefully formed —another habit from her residency, when illegible notes could mean the difference between proper care and a medical error. "Have you considered taking a safety course? The county extension office offers them twice a year."

"Might not be a bad idea," Earl admitted. "Been using them things for forty years, but they keep making 'em more powerful. Old dog, new tricks, you know?"

Tasha smiled at that. Earl had been one of her first patients when she'd arrived in Sweetgum Meadows, suspicious of the young city doctor who'd come to help their beloved Dr. Leighton during what was supposed to be a temporary arrangement. It had taken three visits before he'd stopped calling her "Miss" and started using "Doc," a small victory that had meant more to her than she'd expected.

The familiar rhythm of patient care should have been soothing, but her shoulders remained tight with tension that had nothing to do with Earl's minor injury. It was the same tension that had followed her from Atlanta General's trauma bay to this quiet clinic where the most exciting emergency was usually a fishing hook through someone's thumb or a child with a suspicious rash that turned out to be poison ivy.

Sometimes, in her darkest moments, Tasha wondered if she was wasting her training here. She'd spent six years learning to handle life-and-death situations, to make split-second decisions under impossible pressure, to be the last line of defense between her patients and death. Now she spent her days treating earaches and writing prescriptions for blood pressure medication.

But then she remembered why she'd left Atlanta, and the guilt would settle back into her chest like a familiar weight.

Dr. Amos Leighton appeared in the doorway, his gray hair catching the fluorescent light. At sixty-eight, he moved with the careful precision of someone who'd spent four decades treating everything from broken bones to broken hearts in Sweetgum Meadows. His kind eyes took in the pristine condition of the exam room, Tasha's color-coded supply organization, and the way she'd already begun sanitizing the surfaces.

"You're thorough," he observed, not for the first time.

"Habit." Tasha disposed of her gloves and washed her hands, counting the required twenty seconds under her breath. One Mississippi, two Mississippi... In the trauma bay, thoroughness meant the difference between life and death. Here, it probably meant the difference between a satisfied patient and an annoyed one, but old habits died hard.

The truth was, organization was one of the few things that still made sense to her. When everything else felt uncertain—her career, her future, her ability to trust her own judgment—she could still create order in small spaces. Supply cabinets arranged by category and frequency of use. Patient files color-coded by urgency. A system for everything, because systems didn't fail the way people did.

Earl stood and shook both their hands. His grip was firm despite the bandaged palm, a working man's handshake that spoke of decades spent building and fixing and growing things. "You take care now, Dr. Tasha. And Doc Leighton, tell Martha I said hello."

"Will do, Earl. Drive safe with that hand."

They watched him leave, his boots echoing down the hallway toward the reception area where Mrs. Peterson, the pharmacist's wife, managed appointments and insurance paperwork with the efficiency of someone who'd been doing the job since before computers existed. Dr. Leighton lingered in the doorway, studying Tasha with the same careful attention he'd given her for the past six months.

She'd learned to read his expressions in that time. The slight furrow between his eyebrows meant he was worried about a patient. The way he rubbed his chin indicated he was thinking through a difficult diagnosis. And the look he was giving her now—thoughtful, almost paternal—meant he was about to say something she didn't want to hear.

"You know," he said finally, "in forty years of practice, I've never had an associate who organized supplies by both type and color."

Tasha's cheeks warmed. "It's more efficient."

"It's impressive." He stepped fully into the room, closing the door behind him with the soft click that meant serious conversation was coming. "Tasha, we need to talk about your position here."

The words she'd been dreading. Tasha sank into the desk chair, suddenly exhausted despite the relatively quiet evening. Outside the small window, spring rain had begun to fall, pattering against the glass like nervous fingers. The sound reminded her of another rainy night six months ago, when she'd sat in her Atlanta apartment staring at her resignation letter and wondering if she was making the biggest mistake of her life.

"You're ending the temporary arrangement," she said, because putting off the inevitable had never been her style.

"I'm offering you a permanent position. Martha's been after me to slow down for years. The heart episode last month was her final warning." He settled into the patient chair, looking older than she'd ever seen him. The minor cardiac event had been a wake-up call for everyone—Sweetgum Meadows without Dr. Leighton was almost unimaginable. "I want you to stay permanently, as my partner initially, and eventually to take over when I'm ready to retire."

"Dr. Leighton—"

"You're exactly what this town needs, Tasha. You're skilled, compassionate, and you understand that small-town medicine is about more than just treating symptoms. You treat the whole person, the whole family."

The compliment should have felt good, but instead it sat heavy in her stomach. He was wrong about her—she wasn't compassionate, she was careful. There was a difference. Compassion required the kind of emotional investment she couldn't afford anymore, not after what had happened in Atlanta.

Tasha stared at her hands, still smelling faintly of antiseptic despite multiple washings. "I'm not sure I'm ready for that kind of responsibility."

It was true, but not for the reasons he probably thought. The technical aspects of running a practice didn't scare her—she'd been managing complex cases since her second year of residency. What terrified her was the idea of being someone's only option, their last hope when everything went wrong. She'd failed at that once before, and the cost had been too high.

"You've been ready since the day you walked in here." Dr. Leighton's voice was gentle but firm. "The question is whether you want it."

Whether she wanted it. Six months ago, the answer would have been an automatic no. Six months ago, she'd been Dr. Natasha Jenkins, emergency medicine resident at one of Atlanta's premier teaching hospitals. She'd had a corner office apartment with a view of the city skyline, a promising career trajectory, and a fiancé who collected surgical accolades like some people collected stamps.

Six months ago, she'd lost a patient.

Dante Williams, seventeen years old, brought in after a car accident on a rainy Tuesday night. Multiple trauma, possible internal bleeding, the kind of case that should have been routine for someone with her training. But she'd been awake for thirty-six hours, running on nothing but caffeine and stubborn determination to prove she could handle whatever the emergency department threw at her.

The presentation had been textbook at first glance—stable vitals, no obvious signs of internal injury, alert and oriented. She'd ordered the standard workup and moved on to the next patient, then the next. It wasn't until his blood pressure started dropping that she'd realized what she'd missed. By then, it was too late.

"You let your emotions cloud your judgment," Brandon had said afterward, his voice cold with disappointment. They'd been standing in the hallway outside the family conference room, where Dante's parents were learning that their son wouldn't be coming home. "This is exactly why you're not cut out for emergency medicine. You care too much, and it makes you second-guess yourself."

Too much. As if caring about her patients was a character flaw rather than the reason she'd gone into medicine in the first place. Brandon, who was supposed to be her family—the only real family she'd ever had after years in the foster system—had turned on her when she needed support most.

"I need time to think," she said finally, dragging herself back to the present.

"Of course. But Tasha, I can't wait forever. If you're not interested, I need to start looking for other options. The town deserves continuity of care."

The weight of expectation settled on her shoulders like a lead blanket. An entire community depending on her, trusting her to be there when they needed her most. The thought made her chest tight with familiar anxiety.

After he left, Tasha sat alone in the exam room, listening to the rain intensify against the window. The clinic felt impossibly quiet after the constant noise of the emergency department. No monitors beeping, no overhead pages calling doctors to traumas, no controlled chaos that had once made her feel vital and necessary.

Here, the silence was almost oppressive. It left too much room for thinking, for remembering, for the kind of self-reflection she'd spent six months trying to avoid.

She gathered her things slowly, checking and double-checking that everything was in its proper place. The exam table was wiped down and covered with fresh paper. Supplies were restocked and organized. The small sink was spotless, the soap dispenser full. Order from chaos, the way she'd been taught in medical school.

After turning off the lights and locking up the clinic, Tasha stepped out into the spring evening. The air was cool and damp, carrying the scent of blooming dogwoods and the promise of real warmth to come. Her small apartment above Peterson's Pharmacy was only three blocks away, but she'd learned to love these evening walks through downtown Sweetgum Meadows.

The town was picture-perfect in the way that made city dwellers nostalgic for places they'd never actually lived. Brick storefronts lined Main Street, their windows glowing with warm light. Miller's Hardware still had the same hand-painted sign it had worn for fifty years. The courthouse square sat in the middle of it all, complete with a gazebo where summer concerts drew families with blankets and picnic baskets.

Rochelle's Old-Fashioned Diner anchored one corner, still busy with the dinner crowd despite the rain. Through the windows, Tasha could see families gathered around red vinyl booths, sharing meals and conversation in the easy way of people who'd known each other for decades. It was nothing like the sterile efficiency of the hospital cafeteria, where doctors grabbed quick meals between cases and conversation was limited to shop talk.

Everything about Sweetgum Meadows was the opposite of Atlanta, and that was exactly what Tasha had needed six months ago. The question was whether it was still what she needed now.

Her phone buzzed as she climbed the stairs to her apartment. Brandon's name appeared on the screen, and her stomach clenched with familiar anxiety. She let it go to voicemail, just as she had for the past week. She wasn't ready to hear his voice, wasn't ready to face the reminder of everything she'd left behind.

Inside her small but comfortable apartment, Tasha kicked off her shoes and poured herself a glass of sweet tea from the pitcher she kept in the refrigerator. The space was efficiently organized, much like the clinic, with everything in its proper place. Clean lines, neutral colors, nothing that would remind her of the life she'd abandoned in Atlanta.

She'd furnished it from the local thrift stores and antique shops, finding a strange comfort in things that had belonged to other people, that carried stories she would never know. The dining table had probably hosted decades of family dinners. The rocking chair by the window had likely soothed countless crying babies. There was something peaceful about being surrounded by objects that had witnessed so much life, so much ordinary happiness.

The voicemail notification blinked insistently on her phone. Finally, knowing she couldn't avoid it forever, she played it.

"Tasha, it's me. I know you're avoiding my calls, but we need to talk. There's a position opening in the cardiac surgical unit —research track, stable hours, everything you've always wanted. Dr. Morrison specifically asked for you. This is your chance to come home and get your career back on track. Call me."

Your career. As if the life she was building here was somehow less valid than the one she'd left behind. As if trading the constant pressure of life-and-death decisions for the quiet satisfaction of family medicine made her a failure.

The betrayal still cut deep. Brandon had been the only family she'd ever known—they'd met during her residency, and she'd thought she'd finally found someone who understood her drive to heal, her need to matter. Growing up in foster care had left her hungry for belonging, for someone who would choose her every day. She'd thought Brandon was that person.

Instead, when her world fell apart after Dante Williams' death, when she'd needed support and understanding most, he'd made it clear that her grief was inconvenient. Her guilt was unprofessional. Her trauma was a career liability that reflected poorly on him.

He'd never understood that for Tasha, medicine had always been about something simpler: helping people heal. The fact that she'd failed at that—spectacularly, tragically—was something she wasn't sure she'd ever be able to forgive herself for.

Tasha deleted the message and turned off her phone.

The rain was coming down harder now, drumming against her windows with increasing urgency. She settled onto her couch with a medical journal, but the words blurred together. Her mind kept drifting to Dr. Leighton's offer, to Brandon's message, to the crossroads she'd been avoiding for weeks.

Stay in Sweetgum Meadows and build a quiet life treating everyday ailments and chronic conditions. Return to Atlanta and try to reclaim the ambitious career she'd walked away from. Both options felt impossible in their own way.

A flash of lightning illuminated the room, followed closely by thunder that rattled the windows. The storm was getting worse, the kind of weather that made people nervous about flooding and power outages. Tasha glanced at the clock—nearly nine—and wondered if she should check the clinic's emergency line. Small towns might be quiet, but weather like this had a way of creating unexpected problems.

Her laptop showed a severe thunderstorm warning for the county, with possible flash flooding and winds up to sixty miles per hour. The kind of storm that sent trees into power lines and turned back roads into rivers. She grabbed her emergency bag —old habits from the trauma bay—and headed for her car. The drive to check on any late patients would give her something to do besides stew over life decisions she wasn't ready to make.

The rain hit her windshield like bullets as she pulled out of her parking space behind the pharmacy. Visibility was terrible, and getting worse by the minute. She should probably turn around and wait it out in her apartment, but something about the intensity of the storm made her nervous. What if someone needed help? What if there was an accident on one of the rural roads where cell service was spotty?

She was halfway to the clinic when her headlights caught the reflective triangles of a road closure sign. The main bridge over Sweetgum Creek was flooded, orange cones blocking access while water rushed over the asphalt. The detour signs pointed toward the county road that curved along the ridgeline—a longer route, but the only way around.

The storm seemed even fiercer out here, away from the town's lights and the false sense of security they provided. Her windshield wipers struggled against the torrential downpour, the rubber blades screeching across glass that couldn't shed water fast enough. She found herself gripping the steering wheel tight enough to make her hands ache, leaning forward as if those extra few inches would help her see through the wall of rain.

This was exactly the kind of weather that sent people to the emergency room with everything from heart attacks brought on by storm stress to car accidents caused by poor visibility. In Atlanta, nights like this meant long shifts and full trauma bays. Here, it hopefully just meant a few nervous calls to the clinic's answering service.

She was thinking about turning around when it happened. A massive oak branch, probably loosened by the wind and heavy with rain, crashed down directly in front of her car. Tasha slammed on the brakes, her sedan skidding sideways on the wet asphalt before coming to a stop mere feet from the fallen tree.

Heart pounding, she sat in the sudden silence, rain drumming on her roof while she assessed the situation. The branch completely blocked the narrow road, easily four feet in diameter and stretching from the drainage ditch on one side to the guardrail on the other. There was no way around it, no way to move it, no way forward.

She tried to reverse, but when she turned the key, the engine sputtered and died. Then died again. The electrical storm had apparently found her car's ignition system, or maybe the impact had jarred something loose. Either way, she was stuck.

"Perfect," she muttered, reaching for her phone. No signal, of course. The storm had probably knocked out cell towers throughout the county.

Another lightning flash revealed a gravel driveway about fifty yards back, leading toward a distant light that glowed warm and yellow through the rain. A farmhouse, probably, with people who might have a working phone or at least shelter until the storm passed.

Tasha grabbed her emergency bag and rain jacket, took a deep breath, and stepped out into the storm.

The rain soaked through her jacket immediately, despite its supposed waterproof rating. The wind threatened to knock her sideways, and within seconds she was drenched to the skin, her scrubs clinging uncomfortably and her hair escaping from its careful ponytail. She half-ran, half-stumbled down the gravel drive toward what looked like a large barn, following the sound of her own footsteps on wet stone.

As she got closer, she could hear sounds that didn't belong in an empty building—low moaning, shuffling, and an occasional sharp grunt of distress. Animal sounds, she realized. Someone was dealing with livestock trouble in the middle of the storm.

The barn door was slightly ajar, warm light spilling out into the storm like a beacon. Tasha approached cautiously and peered inside, not wanting to startle whoever was working with the animals.

What she saw made her forget about her own discomfort entirely.

A large brown and white cow lay on her side in a stall filled with fresh straw, clearly in labor and equally clearly in distress. The animal's breathing was rapid and shallow, her sides heaving with effort that wasn't producing results. Tasha could see the problem immediately—a breech presentation, with what looked like a trapped leg preventing normal delivery.

She'd never delivered a calf, but she'd delivered plenty of babies, and the basic principles were the same. More importantly, this animal was suffering, and there was no one else around to help. The farmer was probably in the house, waiting for the veterinarian or trying to figure out what to do.

Tasha set down her bag and assessed the situation with the same methodical approach she'd used in the trauma bay. There was a clean water source, basic veterinary supplies, and even surgical gloves in a plastic container mounted on the wall. Someone had prepared for this emergency, but where were they?

The cow moaned again, a sound of pure distress that cut straight through Tasha's professional reserve. She couldn't just stand here and watch an animal suffer, even if it wasn't technically her area of expertise. The principles were the same— assess, stabilize, intervene when necessary.

She rolled up her sleeves, pulled on the gloves, and approached the laboring cow slowly, speaking in the same calm, reassuring voice she'd used with frightened patients in the trauma bay.

"Easy, girl. Let's see what we can do to help you."

The cow's eyes were wide with pain and exhaustion, but she seemed to calm slightly at the sound of a human voice. Tasha positioned herself carefully, running through everything she knew about difficult deliveries. The breach presentation meant the calf was coming backwards, which could cause complications if the head became trapped. But if she could help reposition things, guide the delivery along...

Thunder crashed overhead, shaking the barn's metal roof and making the single light bulb sway on its cord. In the distance, barely audible over the storm, she could hear the sound of an engine approaching. Headlights appeared through the rain, growing brighter as they turned down the gravel drive.

Help was coming, but Tasha was already committed. The cow's life—and her calf's—might depend on the next few minutes, and she was the only one here to help.

She took a deep breath, centered herself the way she'd learned during her residency, and got ready to do what she'd trained her entire adult life to do: save a life.

Outside, the storm raged on, but inside the warm barn, Dr. Tasha Jenkins found herself exactly where she needed to be.

CHAPTER TWO

The sound of rain hammering against his bedroom window had pulled Grayson Mitchell from restless sleep just after ten o'clock. He'd been dozing fitfully since nine, knowing from five years of experience that weather like this meant emergency calls were coming.

The dream had been the same one that visited him every time storms rolled through—the convoy, the explosion, the screaming of twisted metal and men. He could still taste the dust and blood, still feel the way time seemed to slow in those crucial seconds when everything went wrong. In the dream, he was always too late, always one step behind disaster, always watching helplessly as the people he was supposed to protect slipped away.

Four years since Afghanistan. Four years since the roadside bomb that had flipped their Humvee and left three of his unit dead while he walked away with nothing more than a dislocated shoulder and survivors' guilt that followed him like a shadow. Most days, he could push the memories aside, focus on his work and the quiet life he'd built here in Sweetgum Meadows. But storms like this one brought it all back—the metallic taste of fear, the way thunder sounded too much like incoming artillery, the helpless feeling of being caught in forces beyond his control.

Even as he'd pulled on his clothes and boots, even as he'd checked his veterinary kit and loaded his truck, the familiar tightness in his chest had begun. Storm sounds did that to him, made his hands shake just slightly and his breathing go shallow until he could force himself through the exercises that brought him back to the present.

Four counts in, hold for four, four counts out. Box breathing, they called it. Simple enough that he could do it anywhere —in his truck, in a barn, in the middle of a nightmare that felt too much like memory.

The evening check on his rescue animals had been routine until the storm intensified. He'd established this schedule specifically to combat nights when the weather or his dreams threatened to pull him under. The animals gave him something immediate and necessary to focus on, something that mattered beyond his own struggles.

The three-legged dog named Courage hobbled over when Grayson stepped onto the porch, tail wagging despite the storm raging outside. Grayson had found him two years ago, hit by a car and left for dead on the side of the county road. The local shelter couldn't afford the surgery to save him, so Grayson had done it himself, spending three sleepless nights nursing the animal back to health.

"Easy, boy," he murmured, scratching behind the dog's ears as lightning flickered overhead. "Storm's got you spooked, doesn't it?"

Courage pressed against his legs, seeking comfort. Animals always knew when he was struggling, responding to the tension in his voice and movements with the kind of unconditional support that humans rarely offered. It was one of the reasons he'd chosen veterinary medicine over human healthcare after his discharge—animals didn't ask questions he couldn't answer, didn't expect him to explain why some nights he woke up with his heart racing from dreams he couldn't escape.

Next was Stevie, the blind cat who'd learned to navigate by sound and scent. She purred when he checked her food bowl, rubbing against his ankles despite the wind howling around the barn. He'd found her as a kitten, eyes destroyed by infection, abandoned in a cardboard box behind the veterinary clinic where he'd done his externship.

"There you go, girl," he said as she wound around his feet, seeking the familiar comfort of routine even as the storm raged.

Last was Redemption, the ancient gelding who'd been hours away from slaughter when Grayson found him at a livestock auction three years ago. The horse was twenty-five years old, arthritic, with a sweet temperament that had been his downfall —he was too gentle for riding, too old for breeding, useful only for the meat market until Grayson had stepped in.

"Easy there, old man," Grayson said, checking the horse's water and hay as thunder crashed overhead. "Just a storm, nothing more."

Redemption nickered softly, pressing his gray muzzle against Grayson's shoulder. The horse had been skittish about loud noises when Grayson first brought him home, probably from years of rough handling. Now he was calm most of the time, but storms still made him anxious.

"I know how you feel," Grayson said quietly, running his hand along the horse's neck. "But we're safe here. Just noise, nothing more."

The words were as much for himself as for Redemption. He'd learned to talk to the animals when the silence became too oppressive, when his own thoughts grew too loud to ignore. They listened without judgment, accepted his presence without demanding explanations he couldn't give.

His phone rang just as he was finishing the evening check. Earl Whitaker's name appeared on the screen, and Grayson's chest tightened with anticipation. Earl didn't call this late unless there was real trouble.

"Doc Mitchell?" Earl's voice was tight with worry. "I hate to bother you in this weather, but I've got a problem out here. Bessie's been in labor for hours, and something ain't right. Can you make it out in this mess?"

Grayson was already heading back toward his truck. "What's she showing?"

"Been pushing hard, but nothing's coming. She's getting tired, and I can see something's not positioned right. Looks like the calf might be coming backwards."

Breech presentation. Challenging under the best circumstances, potentially fatal if not handled properly. And in this weather, with roads flooding and visibility near zero, getting there was going to be half the battle.

"I'm on my way," Grayson said, grabbing his emergency kit from the truck. "Keep her as comfortable as you can, but don't try to help with the delivery until I get there. Sometimes it's better to wait."

"Appreciate it, Doc. Drive careful now—these roads are getting nasty."

The drive to Earl's farm was treacherous. Grayson's truck was built for this kind of thing—four-wheel drive, high clearance, good tires—but even so, he had to take it slow. His headlights cut through sheets of rain that reduced visibility to mere yards, and more than once he had to creep around fallen branches or standing water that threatened to flood his engine.

The whole time, he kept his breathing steady and his mind focused on the task ahead. Breech deliveries were tricky but manageable if you caught them early enough. Earl was an experienced farmer who knew when to call for help—if he was worried, there was good reason to be.

The familiar rhythm of emergency response helped calm his storm-triggered anxiety. This was something he knew how to do, something he was good at. Focus on the animal, follow his training, trust his instincts. The same skills that had made him a good medic in Afghanistan, before everything went wrong.

The rain seemed to intensify as he turned onto Earl's gravel drive, his truck's tires fighting for traction on the slick stone. Through the storm, he could see the barn's yellow light glowing warm and steady, a beacon in the chaos of wind and water.

What he hadn't expected was to find someone else already there.

As he parked and grabbed his kit, Grayson could see a figure moving inside the barn, silhouetted against the light. Someone was with Bessie, and from their posture and movements, they knew what they were doing.

"Easy there, Bessie. I'm coming," he called out as he pushed through the barn door, rain dripping from his jacket and boots.

The woman kneeling beside the cow looked up as he approached, and Grayson felt something shift in his chest that had nothing to do with storm-induced anxiety. She was beautiful, yes, but more than that—there was a competence in her eyes, a steadiness that spoke of someone who'd handled emergencies before. Her hands were gloved and positioned properly, her voice calm as she spoke to the laboring animal.

"Are you okay, miss?" he asked, taking in her soaked clothes and the emergency bag beside her.

"I'm fine," she said quickly, not moving from her position beside the cow. "My car broke down on the road, and I heard her in distress. I'm a doctor—human medicine, but I've delivered babies before."

Relief flooded through him. Not just because she was clearly competent, but because something about her presence made the barn feel less lonely, less isolated against the storm. "Dr. Grayson Mitchell," he said, already moving toward the supplies mounted on the wall. "I'm the veterinarian Earl called. Looks like you've already assessed the situation."

"Breech presentation with what appears to be a retained foreleg," she said, falling easily into clinical language that felt like coming home. "She's been pushing for a while, but nothing's progressing."

The assessment was exactly right, matching what Earl had described over the phone. More than that, her positioning beside the cow showed she understood how to help without getting in the way, how to provide support without interfering with the natural process.

"That's exactly what Earl described when he called," Grayson said, pulling on examination gloves with practiced movements. "He went to get his generator going—power's out all over the county." He looked at her, taking in the confident way she held herself. "Good thing you were here. Bessie doesn't usually have problems, but when they do happen..."

"Time matters," she finished.

"Exactly." Something passed between them in that moment—recognition, maybe, of shared understanding. Here was someone who understood that medicine, whether human or animal, was about more than just technical skill. It was about being present in moments of crisis, about caring enough to act when action was needed.

"I'm going to need to reposition the calf," he said, his hands gentle as he examined the cow. "Can you help me keep her calm?"

"Of course."

Working together felt surprisingly natural, like they'd been a team for years rather than strangers meeting in the middle of a crisis. She positioned herself at Bessie's head, murmuring reassurances while keeping the cow calm and steady. Grayson found himself explaining what he was doing as he worked to correct the calf's position—partly for her benefit, but mostly because something about her presence made him want to share his knowledge.

"There," he said finally, feeling both front legs in the correct position. "I can feel both front legs now. On the next contraction—"

Bessie tensed, and Grayson guided the delivery with careful pressure, his training taking over as muscle memory kicked in. The calf slid into the world with a wet rush, landing on the clean straw with a soft thud that seemed impossibly loud in the sudden quiet.

For a heartbeat, the barn was silent except for the rain on the roof. Then the calf lifted its head and let out a wavering bleat that filled the space with the sound of new life.

"There we go," Grayson said, grinning as he cleared the calf's airways and checked its breathing. "Welcome to the world, little one."

The doctor was smiling back at him, and something warm unfurled in Grayson's chest that had nothing to do with professional satisfaction. "Is it always this satisfying?"

"When it goes right? Yeah." He was already moving through his post-delivery checklist, but part of his attention remained on the woman beside him. "This little guy's going to be just fine. Strong as his mama."

Bessie had turned to nuzzle her baby, the soft sounds of maternal bonding filling the barn with a peace that made Grayson's lingering storm anxiety fade completely. This was why he'd chosen veterinary medicine—moments like this, when everything went right and new life entered the world safely.

Earl appeared in the doorway just then, shaking rain from his jacket and grinning at the sight of the healthy calf. "Well, I'll be. Looks like this little one decided not to wait for the storm to pass."

"Stormy," the doctor said with a smile. "Seems fitting, given the circumstances."

"Stormy it is," Earl agreed, moving to examine the calf with obvious pride. "He looks good. Strong."

"He is," Grayson confirmed. "Should be up and nursing within the hour. Keep an eye on them tonight, but I don't anticipate any problems."

As Earl fussed over the newborn and asked about the doctor's car trouble, Grayson learned her name—Dr. Tasha Jenkins, the same Dr. Jenkins he'd heard about around town, the one filling in for Dr. Leighton. He'd wondered when he might meet her, but he'd never imagined it would be like this.

After Earl headed back to the house and they settled in to wait out the storm, Grayson found himself looking forward to the conversation ahead. There was something about Dr. Tasha Jenkins that made him want to know more—about her medical background, about what had brought her to Sweetgum Meadows, about the competence and quiet strength he'd witnessed tonight.

Outside, the storm raged on, but inside Earl's barn, with new life breathing softly in the straw and the promise of getting to know this remarkable woman better, Grayson felt something he hadn't experienced in a long time.

Peace.

CHAPTER THREE

asha had barely slept.

She'd lain awake in her small apartment above the pharmacy, listening to the storm gradually fade into gentle rain, replaying every moment in Earl's barn. The competent way Grayson had handled the delivery. The warmth in his eyes when he'd smiled at her. The easy way they'd worked together, like they'd been partners for years rather than strangers meeting in a crisis.

Most of all, she kept thinking about how right it had felt to be helping again, to be using her skills for something that ended well. It had been months since she'd felt that kind of professional satisfaction, that sense of purpose that had originally drawn her to medicine.

By six in the morning, she'd given up on sleep entirely. She showered, braided her hair into a neat crown around her head, and dressed in navy scrubs and comfortable shoes. The morning was clear and cool, the air washed clean by the storm. Evidence of the night's fury was everywhere—fallen branches, standing water in the low spots, power lines down on the edge of town where crews were already working to restore service.

The pharmacy below her apartment was still closed, but she could hear Elizabeth Peterson moving around in the back room, preparing for the day. Elizabeth had been her landlord and unofficial town guide since she'd arrived in Sweetgum Meadows, a no-nonsense woman in her fifties who seemed to know everyone's business and wasn't shy about sharing her opinions.

Tasha made her way downstairs, drawn by the smell of coffee and the promise of company. She'd learned that Elizabeth was usually the first person awake on Main Street, arriving at the pharmacy before dawn to handle deliveries and prepare medications for the day's pickup.

"Morning, honey," Elizabeth called from behind the prescription counter. "Heard you had quite an adventure last night."

Tasha paused in the doorway. "How did you—"

"Earl called about an hour ago, checking to make sure you got home safe." Elizabeth emerged from the back room with two steaming mugs of coffee. "Said you and Dr. Mitchell made quite a team delivering that calf."

"News travels fast around here," Tasha said, accepting the coffee gratefully.

"Faster than you might like," Elizabeth said with a knowing smile. "Especially when it involves our mysterious veterinarian and the pretty new doctor everyone's been trying to figure out."

"Mysterious?"

Elizabeth settled onto the stool behind the counter, studying Tasha over her coffee mug. "Grayson Mitchell's been here five years, and I could count on one hand the number of times I've seen him in town for anything that wasn't work-related. Keeps to himself, that one. Polite as anything when you run into him, but he doesn't exactly encourage conversation."

Tasha thought about the man she'd worked beside the night before—calm, competent, with kind eyes and gentle hands. There had been something guarded about him, a careful distance that spoke of someone who'd learned to protect himself. She recognized it because she'd been wearing the same armor for months.

"Maybe he's just private," she suggested.

"Maybe." Elizabeth's tone suggested she thought there was more to it. "Or maybe he's been waiting for the right person to draw him out of that shell. Earl seemed to think you two worked together like you'd been doing it for years."

Heat crept up Tasha's neck. "We just happened to be in the right place at the right time."

"Mmm-hmm." Elizabeth's expression was entirely too knowing. "Well, happens Earl mentioned Dr. Mitchell was planning to stop by Malakai's this morning for coffee and breakfast. Apparently delivering calves works up an appetite."

The suggestion hung in the air between them, as subtle as a brick through a window. Tasha found herself fighting a smile. "Are you trying to play matchmaker, Elizabeth?"

"Who, me?" Elizabeth's innocent expression didn't fool anyone. "I'm just passing along information. What you do with it is entirely up to you."

Tasha finished her coffee and headed for the door, calling over her shoulder, "I'm going to pretend you never said anything about the diner."

"Course you are, honey. Course you are."

The walk to the clinic took her right past Rochelle's Old-Fashioned Diner, and despite her protests to Elizabeth, Tasha found herself slowing as she approached. Through the windows, she could see the morning regulars settling into their usual booths—farmers in for coffee before heading to the fields, shop owners grabbing quick breakfasts before opening their doors.

And there, at a small table near the window, was Grayson Mitchell.

He looked different in daylight, less like the rain-soaked

emergency responder and more like a man enjoying a quiet morning meal. His hair was neatly combed, his shirt pressed, and he was reading what looked like a veterinary journal while working his way through a stack of pancakes.

The sight of him made something flutter in her chest, a warmth that had nothing to do with the morning sunshine. Before she could talk herself out of it, she pushed through the diner's door.

The bell above the entrance chimed, and several heads turned in her direction. Tasha felt the weight of curious gazes as she made her way toward Grayson's table, aware that half the diner was probably already composing the story they'd tell their friends about the new doctor and the handsome veterinarian.

"Mind if I join you?" she asked when she reached his table.

Grayson looked up from his journal, and his face lit up with a smile that made her knees slightly weak. "Dr. Jenkins. Please, sit. I was hoping I'd run into you today."

"Tasha," she corrected, sliding into the seat across from him. "After last night, I think we're past the formal titles."

"Tasha," he repeated, and she liked the way her name sounded in his deep voice. "How are you feeling this morning? Any worse for wear after your adventure?"

"Just tired. I kept thinking about last night—about Stormy and Bessie and how well everything went." She paused as Aimee, who ran the diner with her husband Malakai, appeared with a coffee pot and a welcoming smile.

"Well, if it isn't our newest hero," Aimee said, filling a mug for Tasha. "Honey, the whole town's buzzing about what you and Dr. Mitchell did last night."

Tasha glanced around the diner, suddenly aware that the conversations at nearby tables had gotten quieter, as if people were straining to overhear. "We just helped with a difficult birth. It's not exactly heroic."

"Modest, too," Aimee said with approval. "I like that in a

person. You want your usual breakfast, Dr. Mitchell? And what about you, honey?"

"Just coffee for now," Tasha said, still feeling self-conscious about the attention.

"The usual sounds good," Grayson confirmed.

After the waitress moved away, Grayson leaned forward slightly, lowering his voice. "Fair warning—you're about to become the subject of intense community interest. Sweetgum takes its excitement where it can find it, and two medical professionals saving a life in the middle of a storm is pretty much the most interesting thing that's happened here in months."

"Is that your polite way of telling me the entire town is going to be gossiping about us?"

"Pretty much." His smile was rueful but amused. "Hope you don't mind having your private life become public property."

Before Tasha could respond, her phone buzzed against the table. Brandon's name appeared on the screen, and her stomach immediately clenched with familiar anxiety. She declined the call, but not before Grayson noticed her reaction.

"Everything okay?"

"Ex-fiancé," she said shortly. "He's been calling all week."

Something shifted in Grayson's expression, a careful neutrality that told her he was trying not to react to that information. "Sounds complicated."

"It doesn't have to be." The words came out more forcefully than she'd intended. "I left Atlanta for good reasons. I'm not interested in going back."

"Atlanta's loss is Sweetgum's gain, then."

The simple statement, delivered without artifice or obvious flattery, made warmth spread through her chest. When was the last time someone had made her feel valued for who she was rather than what she could do for them?

Aimee reappeared with a plate of eggs, turkey bacon, and

toast for Grayson, along with a slice of pie that looked home-made. "Dr. Mitchell's got a sweet tooth," she explained to Tasha with a conspiratorial wink. "Apple cinnamon pie for breakfast. I keep telling him it's not exactly a balanced meal."

"Life's too short for bad pie," Grayson said, cutting into the slice with obvious enjoyment. "Besides, apples are fruit. That makes it practically health food."

Tasha found herself laughing, the sound surprising her with its genuineness. "That's some creative nutritional reasoning."

"I'm full of creative reasoning. It's one of my many talents."

The easy banter felt natural in a way that caught Tasha off guard. She'd forgotten what it was like to talk to someone without constantly editing herself, without worrying about saying the wrong thing or revealing too much. With Brandon, every conversation had felt like a performance, a careful dance around his ego and expectations.

"What other talents should I know about?" she asked, then immediately felt her face flush at how flirtatious that sounded.

If Grayson noticed, he was too much of a gentleman to comment on it. "Well, I'm pretty good with animals, obviously. I can fix most things that break on a farm. And I make excellent coffee."

"Modest, too," Tasha said, echoing Aimee's earlier comment.

"I have my moments."

The diner's bell chimed again, and Tasha looked up to see a group of women entering together, all of them appearing to be around her age. They spotted her immediately, and after a brief whispered conference, one of them approached the table.

"Excuse me," the woman said with a bright smile. "You must be Dr. Jenkins. I'm Brandi Astore—I'm the head-teacher at the daycare. We heard about last night."

Tasha glanced at Grayson, who was trying unsuccessfully to hide his amusement. "News really does travel fast here."

"Lightning speed," agreed another woman who'd joined

them. "I'm Courtney Matthews. I work with my husband at Justin Time Watch Repair."

"Joanne Richards," said a third woman with stylish shoulder-length hair. "I run the coffee shop down the street."

"And I'm Nevaeh Carr," said the last woman, who had the same warm smile as the others. " I do event planning."

"It's nice to meet you all," Tasha said, genuinely meaning it. The women seemed friendly and welcoming, without the artificial politeness she'd sometimes encountered in Atlanta's medical community.

"We were wondering," Brandi said, "if you'd like to join our book club. We meet Monday evenings here at Rochelle's, and we're always looking for new members."

"It's really more of a social club," Courtney added. "We pick a book, but mostly we end up talking about everything except what we're supposed to be reading."

"Sounds like my kind of book club," Tasha said, surprising herself. She hadn't joined any social groups since arriving in Sweetgum Meadows, hadn't felt ready to put down those kinds of roots.

"Wonderful," Nevaeh said. "Monday at seven. Rochelle's makes the best desserts, so come hungry."

After they moved to their own table, chattering excitedly among themselves, Grayson raised an eyebrow. "Book club, huh? You're really committing to the small-town experience."

"Apparently so." Tasha was still processing the interaction, the easy way the women had welcomed her into their circle. "They seem nice."

"They are. Good people, all of them. Though fair warning—with that group, your social calendar is about to get a lot busier."

"Is that a bad thing?"

Grayson considered the question seriously. "Depends on what you're looking for. If you want to blend into the background and keep to yourself, then yes, it's probably a bad thing. But if you're ready to be part of a community..."

"I might be," Tasha said softly, surprising herself with the admission. "I've been keeping to myself for months, and I'm starting to think that might not be what I need anymore."

"What do you think you need?"

The question was gentle, without pressure or judgment. Tasha found herself really considering it, looking past her automatic defenses to the truth underneath.

"Connection, maybe," she said finally. "Purpose that goes beyond just getting through each day. The feeling that I'm building something rather than just hiding from something."

"Last night felt like building something," Grayson said quietly.

"It did." Their eyes met across the table, and Tasha felt that flutter again, stronger this time. "It felt like the first step toward something good."

Grayson's phone buzzed against the table, and he glanced at it with a slight frown. "Farm call," he said apologetically. "Mrs. Henderson's goat is having some kind of emergency."

"Go," Tasha said. "Duty calls."

He stood, pulling money from his wallet and leaving it on the table. "This was nice. I'm glad you stopped by."

"Me too."

"Maybe we could do it again sometime? Coffee, I mean. Or dinner. Whatever you'd be comfortable with."

The careful way he phrased it, giving her an easy out if she wasn't interested, made her chest tight with something that might have been affection. "I'd like that. Dinner sounds good."

His smile was radiant. "I'll call you. Or rather, I'll figure out how to call you, since I just realized I don't have your number."

"Dr. Leighton's office," Tasha said. "They can reach me anytime."

"I'll remember that."

After he left, Tasha sat in the diner nursing her coffee and thinking about the morning's events. The easy conversation, the warmth in Grayson's eyes, the friendly welcome from the book club women—it all felt like pieces of a life she could actually want, rather than one she was simply enduring.

Her phone buzzed again. Another call from Brandon that she let go to voicemail.

Whatever he wanted, whatever promises or threats or manipulations he was preparing, they belonged to a version of herself she was ready to leave behind. She was building something new here in Sweetgum Meadows, something that felt real and honest and good.

And for the first time in months, she was looking forward to what came next.

CHAPTER FOUR

The morning air carried the scent of fresh hay and the earthy smell of turned soil as Grayson made his rounds through the countryside surrounding Sweetgum Meadows. His truck bounced along the gravel road, veterinary kit rattling softly in the back seat. These daily calls were the backbone of his practice—routine check-ups, vaccinations, the occasional emergency that pulled him from sleep in the middle of the night.

But today felt different. Today, his mind kept drifting back to the woman he'd shared breakfast with just two hours ago.

Tasha Jenkins. Even her name had a musical quality that made him want to say it again. The way she'd laughed at his pie-for-breakfast logic, the gentle teasing in her voice, the momentary vulnerability when she'd talked about her ex-fiancé—all of it played on repeat in his head like a favorite song he couldn't stop humming.

His first stop was Mrs. Henderson's goat farm, where he quickly treated a stone lodged in a hoof—routine work that his hands could manage while his mind wandered. Mrs. Henderson, like everyone else in town, peppered him with questions about "that pretty new doctor" and how they'd worked together "like partners" the night before.

By the time he finished there, word had clearly spread even further. His phone showed three missed calls and two voicemails, all from clients wanting to schedule appointments and, undoubtedly, fish for gossip about the dramatic calf delivery.

Small towns had their drawbacks, but today he found himself smiling at the obvious interest. Let them talk. He had more important things to focus on—like the fact that he'd managed to ask Tasha to dinner and she'd said yes.

His next stop was Earl's farm to check on Stormy and Bessie. As he pulled into the familiar gravel drive, he could see Earl working near the barn—a man in his element, tending to the animals and land he'd worked for decades.

"Dr. Mitchell!" Earl's voice called from the barn as Grayson got out of his truck. "Come see how our boy's doing!"

Inside the barn, Grayson found Earl crouched beside the stall where Bessie lay contentedly chewing cud while Stormy nursed. The sight made his chest warm with professional satisfaction—both animals looked healthy and content, no signs of complications from the difficult birth.

"Look at that," Earl said proudly. "Strong as his mama, just like you said."

Grayson performed a thorough examination of both animals, checking Stormy's vital signs and making sure Bessie was recovering well from the labor. Everything looked perfect— the calf was alert and active, his coat glossy with good health, and Bessie showed no signs of infection or distress.

"He's perfect," Grayson confirmed, straightening up and pulling off his examination gloves. "You've got yourself a fine calf here, Earl."

"Couldn't have done it without you and Dr. Jenkins," Earl said, his weathered face creasing into a smile. "That woman's got steady hands and a good head on her shoulders. Didn't panic once, even when things got dicey."

A familiar warmth spread through Grayson's chest at the mention of Tasha. "She did good work."

"More than good," Earl said with a knowing look. "You two worked together like you'd been partners for years. Made me think maybe it's time this old farm had some regular medical consultation—for the animals and maybe the people too."

Before Grayson could ask what Earl meant by that, the sound of a car engine drew their attention. Through the barn's open door, they could see a small sedan pulling into the drive, kicking up dust as it came to a stop near the house.

A moment later, a slight figure emerged from the passenger side—a young girl with dark hair pulled back in a ponytail. Even from a distance, Grayson could see the nervousness in her posture, the way she hung back while an older woman got out of the driver's side.

"That's my granddaughter Aria," Earl explained, his voice softening with affection. "Casey's bringing her by to see Stormy. Girl's been asking about him since the moment she heard about the birth."

Grayson had heard about Earl's granddaughter but had never met her. Casey Whitaker was a single mother who worked two jobs to support herself and her daughter after her husband's death in a farming accident two years ago. Earl and his wife Martha helped where they could, but it was still a struggle.

"She's nervous around animals," Earl continued, watching as Casey encouraged Aria to walk toward the barn. "Been that way since her daddy died. Casey thinks it's because David was hurt working with livestock, but I think the girl just needs someone patient to show her it's safe."

Grayson understood. He'd seen it before in children who'd experienced trauma—the world suddenly felt dangerous, unpredictable. Animals, with their size and unpredictable movements, could seem especially threatening to an anxious child.

Casey Whitaker appeared in the barn doorway, her arm around her daughter's shoulders. She was a woman in her late twenties with tired eyes but a warm smile, dressed in the uniform of one of her jobs—he thought it might be the grocery store.

"Hi, Mr. Earl," Casey said. "I hope we're not interrupting. Aria's been asking about the calf since she heard about last night."

"Not interrupting at all," Earl assured her. "Dr. Mitchell was just finishing up his examination. Everything looks perfect."

Casey's gaze shifted to Grayson, and he saw recognition flicker in her eyes. "You must be the veterinarian who saved Stormy. Thank you so much. Daddy's been so proud of that calf."

"Just doing my job," Grayson said modestly. "Though I had excellent help from Dr. Jenkins."

Aria peeked around her mother, her large brown eyes fixed on the stall where Stormy was visible nursing from his mother. Grayson could see the longing in her expression, the desire to get closer warring with obvious anxiety.

"Would you like to meet Stormy?" Grayson asked gently, crouching down to Aria's eye level. "He's very gentle, and I'd be right there with you."

Aria looked up at her mother, who nodded encouragingly. "It's okay, baby. Dr. Mitchell knows all about animals."

The little girl took a tentative step forward, then stopped. "Will he hurt me?"

"No," Grayson said with quiet certainty. "Calves are very gentle creatures. And this one is special—he knows he owes his life to some very brave people who helped him come into the world."

Something in his tone seemed to reassure her. Aria took another step, then another, until she was close enough to see into the stall clearly.

"He's so small," she whispered.

"But growing every day," Grayson said. "Would you like to touch him? I can show you how."

Earl and Casey watched as Grayson slowly, patiently guided Aria through her first real interaction with a farm animal. He explained each step, letting her set the pace, never pushing or hurrying. When Aria finally reached out to touch Stormy's soft coat, her face lit up with wonder.

"He's so warm," she marveled.

"That's how you know he's healthy," Grayson explained. "And look how calm he is with you. Animals can sense when someone has a kind heart."

They spent several more minutes in the barn, with Aria gradually becoming more comfortable around the young calf. By the time they left, she was chattering excitedly about how soft his coat was and asking her grandfather if she could visit again soon.

"That's the most interested she's been in anything since David died," Casey said quietly to Grayson as they watched Earl show Aria around the rest of the barn. "Thank you for being so patient with her."

"She's a sweet kid," Grayson replied. "Just needs someone to show her it's safe to trust again."

Casey's expression grew thoughtful. "You know, there aren't many people who understand that. Most folks just see a scared little girl and try to push her to 'get over it.' But you..." She paused, studying his face. "You get it, don't you? What it's like to be afraid after something bad happens."

Grayson felt his chest tighten. He thought of convoy roads and the sound of explosions, of the way his hands still shook sometimes when loud noises caught him off guard. "Yeah," he said quietly. "I get it."

They stood in comfortable silence for a moment, watching as Aria gained confidence with each interaction. When it was time for them to leave, she ran over to Grayson with a shy smile.

"Thank you for showing me Stormy," she said. "Will you be here next time I visit Grandpa?"

"I'll be around," Grayson promised. "And maybe next time you can help me check on him. Would you like that?"

Aria nodded eagerly, and Grayson felt that familiar warmth that came from making a real connection. As he watched Casey and Aria drive away, Earl came to stand beside him.

"You did good with her," Earl said. "Been a long time since I've seen her that excited about anything."

"She just needed someone to listen," Grayson replied. "To let her go at her own pace."

"Same thing that new doctor did with you, sounds like."

Grayson shot Earl a look, but the older man just grinned. "Don't look at me like that. Whole town's talking about how comfortable you two seemed together. Like you'd found your rhythm."

"We just worked well as a team," Grayson said, but even as he said it, he knew it was more than that. There had been something special about the way he and Tasha had operated together, an instinctive understanding that went beyond professional competence.

"That's exactly what I mean," Earl said with satisfaction. "Sometimes the best partnerships are the ones that feel natural from the start."

As Grayson packed up his equipment and prepared to leave, he found himself thinking about Earl's words. Partnership. It was an interesting way to describe what he'd felt working with Tasha. Not just cooperation or collaboration, but something deeper—a sense of shared purpose, of complementary strengths working toward a common goal.

The idea of working with her again, of combining their skills and knowledge, sent a thrill of anticipation through him. But first, he needed to actually follow through on his promise to call her.

He pulled out his phone and dialed Dr. Leighton's office. The receptionist answered on the second ring.

"Sweetgum Family Clinic, this is Margaret."

"Hi Margaret, this is Dr. Mitchell. I was wondering if I could get Dr. Jenkins' contact information? We worked together on an emergency last night and I wanted to follow up about a potential collaboration."

There was a pause, and he could practically hear Margaret's smile through the phone. "Oh yes, Dr. Mitchell. She mentioned you might call. Let me get her number for you."

A few moments later, armed with Tasha's cell phone number, Grayson found himself staring at the digits on his screen. It had been a long time since he'd felt nervous about calling a woman. He took a deep breath and dialed.

"Hello?" Tasha's voice was warm but slightly cautious—the tone of someone answering an unfamiliar number.

"Tasha, it's Grayson. Grayson Mitchell."

"Grayson." He could hear the smile in her voice now. "I was wondering when you'd call."

"I promised I would," he said, surprised by how easy it felt to talk to her. "About that dinner—are you free tomorrow night? I know a place that serves the best barbecue in three counties."

"Tomorrow night sounds perfect. What time?"

"How about seven? I can pick you up."

"Seven works. I'm in the apartment above Peterson's Pharmacy on Main Street."

"I know the place. I'll see you then."

"Looking forward to it," she said, and the warmth in her voice made his chest tight with anticipation.

After they hung up, Grayson sat in his truck for a moment, a grin spreading across his face. For the first time in years, he was looking forward to more than just getting through another day. He was looking forward to discovering what came next.

And that feeling, rare and precious as it was, made everything else—the financial struggles, the long hours, the isolation he'd grown accustomed to—seem suddenly manageable. Because maybe, just maybe, he wouldn't have to face it all alone anymore.

CHAPTER FIVE

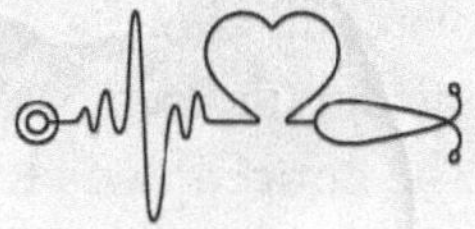

The first book club meeting at Rochelle's Old-Fashioned Diner felt like stepping into a warm embrace. Tasha had arrived a few minutes early, partly from nerves and partly because she'd been looking forward to this all week. The diner buzzed with its usual evening energy—families finishing dinner, teenagers sharing milkshakes, the comfortable hum of a community gathering place.

Malakai, the nephew who'd inherited the diner from his aunt Rochelle, greeted her with a warm smile as she entered. "You must be Dr. Jenkins. The book club ladies have been talking about you all week."

"All good things, I hope," Tasha said, accepting the cup of coffee he offered.

"Nothing but. They're in the back booth—just follow the laughter."

He wasn't kidding. Even from across the diner, Tasha could hear the animated conversation coming from the large corner booth where six women sat surrounded by books, notebooks, and what appeared to be enough dessert for twice their number.

Brandi spotted her first and waved her over with enthusiasm. "Tasha! Perfect timing. We were just arguing about whether the heroine in this month's book is brave or just stupid."

"There's a difference?" Tasha asked, sliding into the booth beside Nevaeh.

"She's going to fit right in," Courtney said with approval. "I like her already."

Joanne pushed a plate of chocolate cake toward Tasha. "Malakai's specialty. Consider it a membership fee."

As Tasha settled in, she noticed two other women she hadn't met at the diner before. "I'm India," one said with a warm smile. "I work at the ice cream parlor. Well, technically my husband Rashad owns it, but I help out between my other job."

"And I'm Mrs. Bridges," the other added. "I teach Sunday school at the Methodist church. These girls keep trying to corrupt me with their romance novels, but I keep coming back for the company."

"Don't let her fool you," Brandi said with a grin. "Mrs. Bridges reads more romance than any of us. She just hides the covers when she's at church."

Mrs. Bridges winked at Tasha. "A lady needs her secrets."

As Tasha settled in, she felt the last of her nervousness fade away. These women had an easy warmth that reminded her why she'd gone into medicine in the first place—the desire to be part of something larger than herself, to contribute to a community.

"So," Brandi said, opening her worn paperback, "newcomer's choice. Brave heroine or foolish one?"

Tasha skimmed the back cover of the romance novel they'd been reading. "Well, if she's falling in love with a mysterious stranger who may or may not be dangerous, I'd say the jury's still out. Depends on her reasons."

"See?" Nevaeh said, pointing her fork at the others. "I told you it was about motivation."

"Everything's about motivation with you," Courtney teased.

"You organize events for a living. You think everyone's motivated by perfect timing and coordination."

"Because they are," Nevaeh shot back. "Speaking of which, when are you going to let my husband Sean teach you to salsa properly? I could organize a private lesson."

"When pigs fly," Courtney said firmly, but Tasha caught the slight smile Courtney tried to hide.

"How is my niece Ebony tonight?" India asked Nevaeh. "Sean managing okay on his own?"

Nevaeh smiled. "She was practically asleep when I left. Sean's got the bedtime routine down to a science now. Though he'll probably text me three times before we're done here asking where I keep the backup pacifiers."

As the conversation flowed around the table, Tasha found herself relaxing in a way she hadn't in months. These women were friends in the truest sense—they teased each other mercilessly but with obvious affection, supported each other's dreams and decisions, and created a space where everyone felt heard.

"Alright, enough about fictional romance," Nevaeh said, fixing Tasha with a pointed look. "Let's talk about real-life romance. Specifically, the very real romance brewing between our newest member and a certain handsome veterinarian."

Tasha nearly choked on her coffee. "I'm sorry, what?"

"Please," Joanne said, rolling her eyes. "Half the town saw you two at breakfast yesterday morning. Word is you were practically glowing."

"And Grayson asked you to dinner," India added. "Mrs. Peterson told my mother-in-law, who told me. When's the big date?"

"Tomorrow night," Tasha admitted, then immediately regretted it as all six women leaned forward with predatory interest.

"Details," Courtney demanded. "Where's he taking you? What are you wearing? Have you kissed him yet?"

"Courtney!" Tasha protested, but she was laughing despite herself.

"What? These are important questions. A woman needs to be prepared."

"Speaking of preparation," Brandi said, pulling out her phone, "we should take you shopping. There's a cute boutique in the next town over that has the perfect dress for a first date."

"I don't need—"

"Yes, you do," all six women said in unison, then burst into laughter.

"It's decided then," Mrs. Bridges declared with authority. "Tomorrow afternoon, we're taking you shopping. Consider it a community service project."

Tasha found herself swept along by their enthusiasm. When was the last time she'd had friends who cared enough to meddle in her love life? In Atlanta, her relationships with colleagues had been cordial but professional. There had been no one to share excitement with, no one to offer advice or just listen when things went wrong.

"You know," she said slowly, "I'd forgotten what it was like to have people who actually care about what happens to me."

The teasing stopped abruptly, and Nevaeh reached over to squeeze her hand. "Well, you've got us now. Whether you want us or not."

"Trust me," Joanne added, "once you're part of this group, you're stuck with us. We're like a benevolent mafia."

"With better desserts," Courtney said, stealing a bite of Tasha's cake.

"And better fashion sense," India added. "Seriously, we are going to find you the perfect outfit tomorrow."

The conversation moved on to other topics—Brandi's latest community center project, Joanne's coffee shop aspirations, Nevaeh's upcoming wedding she was planning for a couple from the next town over—but Tasha found herself only half-listening. Instead, she was absorbing the warmth of belonging, the simple pleasure of being included in the casual intimacy of long friendship.

Her phone buzzed with a text message, and she glanced down to see Grayson's name on the screen. "Looking forward to tomorrow night. Sweet dreams. - G"

The message was simple, but it made her chest flutter with anticipation. She typed back quickly: "Me too. Sleep well."

"Lover boy texting already?" Brandi asked, trying to peek at the phone.

"Maybe," Tasha said, but she couldn't hide her smile.

"She's got it bad," India observed with satisfaction. "Look at that grin."

"I do not have anything bad," Tasha protested, but even she could hear the lack of conviction in her voice.

"Honey," Mrs. Bridges said gently, "there's nothing wrong with having it bad. Sometimes that's exactly what we need to remind us we're alive."

The words hit deeper than Mrs. Bridges probably intended. Tasha had spent so many months just surviving, just getting through each day without thinking about what came next. The idea of wanting something—someone—with real intensity was both thrilling and terrifying.

"What if I mess it up?" she heard herself ask.

The question surprised her. She hadn't meant to voice her fears, but somehow these women had created a space where honesty felt safe.

"Then you mess it up," Brandi said matter-of-factly. "And then you figure out how to fix it, or you learn from it and move on. That's how life works."

"Besides," Joanne added, "from what I saw yesterday morning, that man is just as invested as you are. You don't look at someone the way he was looking at you unless you're already halfway gone."

"How was he looking at me?"

"Like you were the answer to a question he'd been asking for years," Courtney said softly.

The words sent a shiver through Tasha. Was that what she'd seen in his eyes? That sense of recognition, of possibility?

"The point is," Brandi said, "you deserve to take the chance. You deserve to be happy, Tasha. Don't let fear rob you of that."

They spent another hour talking—about books and dreams and the small dramas of small-town life. By the time the meeting wound down, Tasha felt lighter than she had in months. As they prepared to leave, phones started buzzing around the table.

"Emergency at the high school," Brandi said, reading her screen. "Hit-and-run in the parking lot after the basketball game."

"I got the same alert," Courtney said, already standing. "No injuries reported, but they're asking for witnesses."

"We should go," India said. "My cousin was at that game tonight."

"Tasha, you coming?" Nevaeh asked, gathering her purse.

Tasha hesitated. She wasn't officially part of their emergency response network, wasn't sure what help she could offer. But these women had welcomed her so completely tonight, made her feel like she belonged in a way she hadn't experienced in years.

"Let's go," she said, following them out into the night.

The high school parking lot was chaos when they arrived. Police cars with flashing lights, clusters of teenagers and parents talking in urgent whispers, and in the center of it all, a damaged car with its front bumper crumpled and headlight shattered.

The book club women dispersed immediately, each finding their role in the unfolding drama. Brandi went to talk to the police officers, Courtney headed toward a group of her students, and Mrs. Bridges began organizing the parents who were frantically trying to locate their children.

Tasha stood for a moment, uncertain, until she spotted a teenage girl sitting on the curb, holding her arm and crying. Medical instincts kicked in immediately.

"Hey," she said gently, crouching down beside the girl. "I'm Dr. Jenkins. Are you hurt?"

The girl looked up with tearful eyes. "I think I twisted my wrist when I jumped out of the way. It happened so fast—this car just came flying through the parking lot and hit Mrs. Patterson's car. If I hadn't moved..."

"Let me take a look," Tasha said, carefully examining the girl's wrist. It was swollen but didn't appear to be broken. "I think you're going to be fine, but we should get you some ice and maybe have your parents take you for an X-ray just to be sure."

As she helped the girl find her parents and recommended follow-up care, Tasha felt something settle into place inside her chest. This was what she'd been missing—the ability to help, to be useful, to make a difference in someone's day.

When the immediate crisis was handled and the police had finished taking statements, the book club women regrouped in the parking lot.

"Well, that was exciting," Joanne said dryly.

"Poor Mrs. Patterson," Nevaeh said, looking at the damaged car. "At least no one was seriously hurt."

"Thanks to quick reflexes and a guardian angel," Mrs. Bridges added. "Could have been much worse."

As they walked back to their cars, Brandi fell into step beside Tasha. "You were good back there," she said quietly. "Natural instincts for helping people. This town could use more of that."

"I'm just glad I could help," Tasha replied, and meant it.

Back in her apartment later, Tasha reflected on the evening as she got ready for bed. The warmth of the book club, the easy acceptance, the way she'd automatically stepped in to help during the emergency—it all felt like pieces of herself clicking back into place.

Her phone rang, startling her from her thoughts. Brandon's name appeared on the screen, and her good mood evaporated instantly. She let it go to voicemail, just as she had every time he'd called this week.

But this time, curiosity got the better of her. What could he possibly have to say that required such persistence?

She played the voicemail, immediately regretting it as Brandon's familiar voice filled her apartment.

"Tasha, we need to talk. I know you're avoiding my calls, but this is important. There's been a development in the Dante Williams case—his family is asking questions about the care he received. Dr. Morrison thinks it would be better if you came back and helped us present a united front. The hospital is willing to offer you a very generous settlement to put this behind us. Call me back."

The message ended, leaving Tasha staring at her phone in shock. The Dante Williams case—the teenager she'd lost, the patient whose death had driven her from Atlanta. She'd thought that chapter of her life was closed, the investigation complete. The family had been devastated but had seemed to accept that sometimes, despite everyone's best efforts, tragedies happened.

Now Brandon was suggesting there were questions being raised, implications that someone had made mistakes. And he wanted her to come back to help with damage control.

She sank onto her couch, her mind racing. What kind of questions? What had they found? And why did Brandon sound like he was offering her a bribe to keep quiet?

The doubt that had plagued her for months came rushing back. Had she missed something that night? Had her exhaustion and emotional state clouded her judgment in ways she hadn't recognized? Was Dante Williams dead because she hadn't been good enough when it mattered most?

Her hands were shaking as she set the phone aside. The confidence she'd been building, the sense of belonging she'd found here in Sweetgum Meadows, suddenly felt fragile. Maybe Brandon was right. Maybe she was hiding from her responsibilities, running away from consequences she should be facing.

But even as the familiar spiral of self-doubt began, another voice in her head pushed back. Brandon had always been manipulative, always found ways to make her question herself when it served his purposes. And the timing of this call, just as she was building a new life, felt suspiciously convenient.

She thought about Grayson's steady hands delivering Stormy, his patient way with Aria, the warmth in his eyes when he looked at her. She thought about the book club women and their easy acceptance, their belief that she deserved happiness.

Was she going to let Brandon's voice in her head override all of that?

Her phone buzzed with a text from Nevaeh: "Had such a good time tonight! Can't wait to hear all about your date tomorrow. Sweet dreams!"

The simple message of friendship and support made Tasha's eyes well up. This was what she'd been missing in Atlanta—people who cared about her happiness, who believed in her worth as a person rather than just her value as a doctor.

She typed back: "Thank you for welcoming me. See you soon."

Then she turned off her phone and went to brush her teeth, determinedly not thinking about Brandon or Atlanta or the shadows from her past that kept trying to pull her backward.

Tomorrow night, she was having dinner with a man who made her remember what it felt like to hope. Tomorrow night, she was going to take Courtney's advice and not let fear rob her of the chance to be happy.

Everything else could wait.

CHAPTER SIX

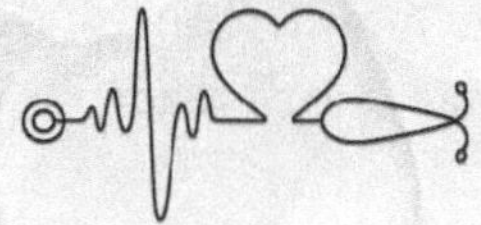

Grayson checked his reflection in the rearview mirror one more time, adjusting his collar. He'd changed shirts three times before settling on the navy button-down that his sister had given him last Christmas, claiming it brought out his eyes. The small bouquet of wildflowers he'd picked from his own property sat on the passenger seat, and he hoped they looked intentional rather than haphazard.

Seven o'clock exactly. He believed in punctuality, especially when it came to something this important.

He knocked on the door to the apartment above Peterson's Pharmacy, his heart beating faster than it had any right to during what should have been a simple dinner date. But nothing about Tasha Jenkins felt simple. From the moment he'd first seen her in Earl's barn, competent and unflappable in the face of a veterinary emergency, she'd occupied his thoughts in ways that both thrilled and unsettled him.

The door opened, and Grayson forgot how to breathe.

Tasha stood before him in a coral dress that skimmed her curves perfectly, her hair styled in soft waves that framed her face. She looked elegant and confident, and the smile she gave him made his chest tight with something that felt dangerously close to awe.

"Hi," he managed, holding out the flowers. "You look... wow."

"Thank you," she said, accepting the bouquet with obvious pleasure. "These are beautiful. Let me just put these in water."

He followed her into the small apartment, noting the medical degree framed on the wall, the stack of books on the coffee table, the way she moved through the space with the easy confidence of someone who'd made it her own despite its temporary nature.

"Emory University School of Medicine," he said, reading the diploma. "Impressive."

"A lifetime ago," Tasha replied, arranging the flowers in a mason jar with practiced efficiency. "Ready?"

The drive to Ruby's Smokehouse took them through countryside that Grayson never tired of—rolling hills dotted with cattle, farmhouses with wide porches, the kind of landscape that reminded him why he'd chosen to build his life here rather than in some sterile suburban practice.

"Tell me about this place we're going," Tasha said, rolling down her window to let in the warm evening air.

"Ruby's Smokehouse," Grayson replied. "About twenty minutes outside town. The owner, Ruby Williams, makes the best barbecue this side of Memphis. It's not fancy, but the food is incredible."

"Sounds perfect. I've been craving good barbecue since I moved here."

"How are you settling in?" he asked, glancing over at her. The evening light caught the highlights in her hair, and he had to force himself to focus on the road. "I know small-town life can be an adjustment."

Tasha was quiet for a moment, and he wondered if he'd touched on something sensitive. "It's different," she said finally. "But different in good ways, mostly. People here actually care about each other. In Atlanta, I could go days without having a real conversation with anyone."

"What made you choose Sweetgum Meadows? It's not exactly a destination most doctors have on their radar."

Another pause, longer this time. "I needed a change," she said, her voice careful. "Sometimes life forces you to reevaluate everything you thought you wanted."

Grayson heard the weight behind her words, the suggestion of pain or disappointment that had driven her here. He understood that feeling intimately—the need to escape, to start over somewhere no one knew your history or your failures.

"I get that," he said quietly. "Sometimes the best decisions are the ones that feel like running away."

She turned to look at him, and he caught the surprise in her expression. "You sound like you speak from experience."

"Maybe I do."

They fell into comfortable silence, the truck's tires humming against the asphalt as they left Sweetgum Meadows behind. Grayson found himself stealing glances at Tasha, noting the way she seemed to relax as they drove, her shoulders dropping and her breathing deepening.

Ruby's Smokehouse appeared around a bend in the road—a low, wooden building with a wraparound porch and smoke rising from a chimney that suggested serious barbecue happening inside. The parking lot was gravel, and pickup trucks outnumbered sedans three to one.

"This is it," Grayson said, pulling into a space near the front door. "I should warn you, Ruby's got opinions about everything, and she's not shy about sharing them."

Tasha laughed. "I think I can handle opinionated restaurant owners."

Inside, the restaurant was exactly what Grayson had hoped —dim lighting, wooden tables scarred by years of use, and the smoky aroma of meat that had been cooking low and slow for hours. A woman in her late sixties with silver hair and sharp eyes approached their table almost immediately.

"Well, well," Ruby said, looking between them with obvious interest. "Dr. Mitchell, you didn't tell me you were bringing company tonight."

"Ruby Williams, meet Dr. Tasha Jenkins," Grayson said. "Tasha, this is Ruby. She owns the place and makes the best beef ribs you'll ever taste."

"Doctor, huh?" Ruby studied Tasha with the intensity of someone sizing up a potential daughter-in-law. "What kind of doctor?"

"Family medicine," Tasha replied smoothly. "I'm working with Dr. Leighton in Sweetgum Meadows."

"About time that man got some help. He's been working himself to death for years." Ruby's approval was evident in her tone. "You picked a good one," she said to Grayson with a wink. "Pretty and smart. Don't mess it up."

"Ruby," Grayson said, his voice tight as he rubbed the back of his neck, fighting the warmth rising in him.

"What? I'm just saying what everyone's thinking." She turned back to Tasha. "This one's been eating dinner alone at my restaurant for three years. Nice to see him finally bring some company."

After Ruby left them with menus and sweet tea, Grayson shook his head. "I'm sorry about that. Ruby's got no filter."

"I like her," Tasha said, grinning. "She reminds me of my grandmother. No nonsense, but you can tell she cares."

They ordered—beef ribs for him, barbecue chicken for her, with sides of mac and cheese and coleslaw to share. As they waited for their food, Grayson found himself studying Tasha's face in the warm light of the restaurant. She looked more relaxed than he'd seen her since they'd met, the tension he'd noticed around her eyes softened.

"So," she said, leaning back in her chair, "Ruby mentioned

you've been eating here alone for three years. Is that how long you've been in Sweetgum Meadows?"

"Five years total," Grayson replied. "I bought the practice from Dr. Harrison when he retired. Ruby's just commenting on how long it's been since I brought a date here."

"And how long has that been?"

The question was asked lightly, but Grayson caught the genuine curiosity underneath. "A while," he said honestly. "I was married before. My wife died four years ago."

Tasha's expression immediately shifted to one of sympathy. "I'm sorry. That must have been incredibly difficult."

"It was. Still is, some days." He'd never talked about Leslie's death easily, but something about Tasha's direct gaze and the safety of this dimly lit restaurant made the words come more readily. "Cancer. We fought it for two years, but in the end..."

"I'm sorry," Tasha said again, reaching across the table to briefly touch his hand. "Losing someone you love that way... it changes everything."

There was something in her tone that made him look at her more closely. "You sound like you understand."

"Not the same way," she said quickly. "I've never lost a spouse. But I understand how one event can reshape your entire life."

Before he could ask what she meant, Ruby appeared with their food, setting down plates piled high with meat that fell off the bone and sides that steamed in the cool evening air.

"Eat up," Ruby commanded. "And don't let it get cold while you're making moon eyes at each other."

The food was as incredible as Grayson had promised, and they spent the next hour eating and talking about easier topics —favorite books, travel dreams, the quirks of small-town life. Tasha had a sharp sense of humor that caught him off guard, and more than once he found himself laughing harder than he had in months.

"So," she said, stealing a bite of his mac and cheese, "what made you want to be a veterinarian? Always love animals?"

"Actually, I wanted to be a human doctor first," Grayson admitted. "Pre-med, full scholarship to college, the whole track. But life had other plans."

"What happened?"

"Iraq happened. I enlisted after 9/11, did two tours as a medic. When I came back..." He paused, choosing his words carefully. "Let's just say working with animals felt like a better fit than working with people."

Tasha nodded slowly. "PTSD?"

"Among other things." He was surprised by how easily he'd admitted that to her. Most people either didn't understand or tried too hard to be understanding. Tasha just accepted it as information. "Animals don't judge. They don't lie. They're honest about what they need and grateful when you help them."

"That's actually beautiful," Tasha said softly. "And from what I saw with Stormy, you're exactly where you're supposed to be."

The sincerity in her voice made his chest tight. "What about you? Always want to be a doctor?"

"Since I was twelve. There was another kid in my foster home who fell and broke his arm badly. The doctor who treated him was so calm and competent, made this scared kid feel safe even though he was in terrible pain and had no family there with him." She paused, her voice growing quieter. "I wanted to be able to do that for people—to be the steady presence when someone has no one else."

"Foster home?" Grayson asked gently.

Tasha's fingers traced the rim of her coffee mug. "I've been in the system for as long as I can remember. Never knew my real family." She shrugged, trying to make it sound casual. "Most of my placements were... fine. Not bad, just not really family either. More like I was a monthly check that came with responsibilities."

"That must have been lonely."

"It was what it was. My foster parents weren't cruel, just not particularly invested. I learned early that I needed to take care of myself." Her voice was matter-of-fact, but Grayson could hear the old hurt underneath. "The day I turned eighteen, I was officially on my own. College, medical school, everything—I did it by myself."

"And did you accomplish your goal? To make them feel safe?" he asked, returning to her earlier comment.

Tasha's smile faltered slightly. "I used to think so. Now I'm not so sure."

There was pain in those words, a story she wasn't ready to tell. Grayson recognized the signs—he'd worn that same guarded expression for months after returning from overseas.

"For what it's worth," he said gently, "you made me feel safe that night in Earl's barn. Capable and calm under pressure."

Her eyes brightened, and she ducked her head as if embarrassed by the compliment. "Thank you. That means more than you know."

They lingered over dessert—bread pudding with bourbon sauce that Ruby insisted they try—and Grayson found himself reluctant for the evening to end. When was the last time he'd enjoyed someone's company this much? When had conversation felt this easy, this natural?

As they drove back toward Sweetgum Meadows, Tasha was quiet beside him, her window cracked to let in the night air. The silence felt comfortable rather than awkward, the kind of companionship that didn't require constant conversation.

"Thank you for tonight," she said as he pulled up in front of the pharmacy. "The food was incredible, and the company was even better."

"Would you like to do it again sometime?" The question came out before he could second-guess himself.

"I'd like that very much."

He walked her to her door, hyperaware of her presence beside him, the light scent of her perfume mixing with the evening air. On her doorstep, they paused, and he found himself stepping closer, drawn by something he couldn't name.

"Grayson," she said softly, and he heard both invitation and uncertainty in her voice.

He reached up to cup her face gently, giving her time to pull away if she wanted to. When she didn't, when she instead stepped closer, he leaned down and kissed her.

It was soft at first, tentative, a question rather than a statement. But when she sighed and melted against him, her hands coming up to rest on his chest, the kiss deepened into something that made his head spin.

When they finally broke apart, both were breathing hard.

"Wow," Tasha whispered.

"Yeah," Grayson agreed, his forehead resting against hers. "Wow."

They stood there for a moment, reluctant to break the connection. Finally, Tasha stepped back, her hand lingering on his chest.

"Good night, Grayson."

"Good night, Tasha."

He waited until she was safely inside before walking back to his truck, his lips still tingling and his heart beating faster than it had in years. As he drove home through the quiet streets of Sweetgum Meadows, Grayson allowed himself to hope that maybe, just maybe, he was ready to let someone in again.

And maybe she was ready to let him in too.

CHAPTER SEVEN

$\mathcal{T}$asha woke to sunlight streaming through her bedroom curtains and the phantom sensation of Grayson's lips on hers. She touched her mouth reflexively, remembering the gentle pressure of his kiss, the way her heart had raced when he'd cupped her face so tenderly on her doorstep.

The memory should have made her smile. Instead, it filled her with a creeping sense of unease.

She'd let herself get carried away last night, swept up in good food and easy conversation and the intoxicating feeling of being truly seen by someone. But in the harsh light of morning, reality was reasserting itself. She was a doctor with a potentially ruined career, hiding in a small town while her past threatened to catch up with her. What right did she have to drag someone as good as Grayson into that mess?

Her phone buzzed on the nightstand. Another voicemail from Brandon, the third this week. She deleted it without listening, but the damage was already done. The anxiety that had been her constant companion for months came flooding back, turning her stomach and making her hands shake.

She was fooling herself if she thought she could just start over, build a new life without dealing with the wreckage of her old one. Brandon's persistent calls were proof that her past wasn't going to stay buried. And when it all came out—when the questions about Dante Williams' death became public— what would Grayson think of her then?

A shower did nothing to wash away her spiraling thoughts. Neither did coffee or the blueberry muffin she forced herself to eat. By the time she dressed for work, Tasha had convinced herself that last night had been a mistake. A beautiful mistake, but a mistake nonetheless.

She was stepping out of her apartment when she nearly collided with Elizabeth Peterson, who was unlocking the pharmacy below.

"Morning, honey," Elizabeth said with a knowing smile. "Heard you had quite the evening. Grayson's truck was parked out here pretty late."

Heat flooded Tasha's cheeks. "Just dinner."

"Mm-hmm. Must have been some dinner, judging by that glow you're wearing."

"I'm not glowing," Tasha protested, but Elizabeth just laughed.

"Honey, I've been watching folks fall in love in this town for twenty years. Trust me, you're glowing."

The word 'love' hit Tasha like a physical blow. Love was the last thing she could afford right now. Love meant vulnerability, meant opening herself up to hurt and disappointment and the possibility that someone else would pay the price for her mistakes.

She mumbled something about being late for work and hurried toward the clinic, Elizabeth's knowing chuckle following her down the street.

The morning at Dr. Leighton's office was mercifully busy. A steady stream of patients kept her mind occupied—routine check-ups, minor injuries, the familiar rhythm of diagnostic work that had always been her anchor. Mrs. Patterson came in for follow-up bloodwork, chattering about the hit-and-run at the high school and how grateful she was that no one had been seriously injured.

"That new book club of yours was quite helpful that night," Mrs. Patterson said as Tasha drew her blood. "Organizing folks, making sure everyone stayed calm. You've got good friends there."

"They're wonderful women," Tasha agreed, trying to ignore the pang of guilt. How could she be part of their group when she was keeping such significant secrets? When she might have to leave Sweetgum Meadows at any moment to deal with the legal fallout from Dante Williams' case?

Dr. Leighton appeared in the doorway as Mrs. Patterson was leaving. "Tasha, do you have a minute? There's something I'd like to discuss."

Her heart immediately started racing. Had he heard something? Had word of her troubles somehow reached Sweetgum Meadows?

But when she followed him into his office, Dr. Leighton's expression was warm rather than concerned.

"I wanted to talk to you about making your position here permanent," he said, settling behind his desk. "You've been a tremendous asset these past few weeks. The patients love you, you've integrated beautifully with the community, and frankly, I could use the help on a long-term basis."

Tasha felt the air leave her lungs in a rush. A permanent position. The security and stability she'd been craving, the chance to truly build a life in Sweetgum Meadows. It was everything she wanted, and it terrified her completely.

"That's very generous," she managed. "Can I think about it?"

Dr. Leighton looked surprised. "Of course. I just assumed... well, you seem so settled here. And there's talk around town about you and Dr. Mitchell. I thought you might be ready to put down roots."

The mention of Grayson made her stomach clench. "It's a big decision. I'd like some time to consider all the implications."

"Take all the time you need. The offer will stand."

Tasha made it through the rest of the morning on autopilot, her mind churning. Dr. Leighton's offer should have been cause for celebration. Instead, it felt like another weight pressing down on her chest, another way she was deceiving good people who trusted her.

During her lunch break, she walked to the small park in the center of town, hoping the fresh air would clear her head. Instead, she found herself thinking about Grayson's hands on her face, the way he'd looked at her like she was something precious and worth protecting.

She was so lost in thought that she didn't notice the approaching footsteps until someone called her name.

"Tasha! There you are."

She turned to find Brandi walking toward her, a wide smile on her face and determination in her step.

"We've been texting you all morning," Brandi said, settling onto the bench beside her. "We want to hear everything about last night. And I mean everything."

"There's not much to tell," Tasha said weakly.

Brandi snorted. "Please. Grayson Mitchell has been walking around town this morning looking like he won the lottery. Don't tell me there's nothing to report."

Despite her anxiety, Tasha felt a flutter of pleasure at that. "He looked happy?"

"Happy? Honey, the man was practically floating. Mrs. Henderson saw him at the feed store, and she said he was humming. Humming, Tasha. She's known him for three years and has never seen him so much as smile before ten AM."

The image of Grayson humming made something warm

unfurl in Tasha's chest, even as the voice in her head reminded her that she had no right to that happiness.

"It was a nice evening," she admitted.

"And? Come on, give me something. Where did he take you? What did you talk about? Did he kiss you goodnight?"

The memory of that kiss sent heat flooding through her. "Brandi..."

"Oh my God, he did! Look at your face! You're blushing like a teenager."

"It's complicated," Tasha said, and the understatement of the century threatened to make her laugh hysterically.

Brandi's expression immediately grew serious. "Complicated how? Did something happen? Did he say something wrong?"

"No, nothing like that. Grayson was perfect. That's the problem."

"I'm not following."

Tasha stared at her hands, trying to find words for the tangle of emotions in her chest. "I'm not in a position to start something serious with anyone right now. There are things about my past, about why I left Atlanta... I'm not ready to explain all of that to someone."

"So don't explain it," Brandi said simply. "Not yet, anyway. Relationships don't come with a timeline, Tasha. You don't have to spill your entire life story on the second date."

"But what if those things affect him? What if my past ends up hurting him somehow?"

Brandi was quiet for a long moment, studying Tasha's face. "You want to know what I think?"

"I think you're scared. And I think you're looking for reasons to run away before someone gets close enough to hurt you."

The words hit uncomfortably close to home. "That's not—"

"Isn't it?" Brandi's voice was gentle but firm. "Look, I don't know what happened in Atlanta. But I know you, at least the version of you that's been living here for the past few months. You're kind and competent and brave. You jumped in to help deliver a calf in the middle of a storm. You joined our book club and our emergency response team without hesitation. That's not the behavior of someone who has something terrible to hide."

"You don't understand—"

"Then help me understand. What could possibly be so bad that it would make Grayson Mitchell, a man who's been alone for four years, not want to take a chance on you?"

Tasha felt tears prick at her eyes. "A patient died. A teenager. And there are questions about whether I could have done something differently, whether I made mistakes that cost him his life."

The words hung in the air between them, and Tasha waited for Brandi's expression to change, for the judgment and disappointment to replace the warmth in her eyes.

Instead, Brandi reached over and took her hand.

"How long had you been on shift when it happened?" she asked quietly.

"Thirty-six hours. I was exhausted, but the ER was swamped, and—"

"Thirty-six hours." Brandi shook her head. "Honey, doctors are human. You can't save everyone, especially when you're being pushed beyond reasonable limits."

"Tell that to his family. Tell that to the lawyers who might be coming after me."

"Is that what this is about? Legal trouble?"

Tasha wiped at her eyes with the back of her hand. "I don't know yet. My ex-fiancé keeps calling, saying there are new questions being raised. He wants me to come back to Atlanta to help with damage control."

"Your ex-fiancé who you've been avoiding?" Brandi's tone

sharpened. "The one who's been harassing you with phone calls all week?"

"He's trying to help—"

"Is he? Or is he trying to manipulate you into coming back for his own reasons?"

"I don't know," she admitted.

"Well, I think you need to figure that out before you make any decisions about your future. And that includes your future with Grayson."

They sat in silence for a few minutes, watching families walk through the park with their children, couples strolling hand in hand. Normal people living normal lives, unburdened by the weight of life-and-death decisions and their consequences.

"Can I ask you something?" Brandi said finally.

Tasha nodded.

"Do you have feelings for Grayson?"

The question was simple, but the answer felt enormous. "Yes," Tasha whispered.

"Real feelings? The kind that scare you because they matter?"

"Yes."

"Then don't let fear rob you of that. Don't let some manipulative ex or a case that may or may not go anywhere steal your chance at happiness."

Tasha's phone buzzed in her pocket. Another call from Brandon. This time, instead of letting it go to voicemail, she answered.

"What do you want, Brandon?"

"Tasha, thank God. We need to talk. Can you be back in Atlanta by this weekend? The hospital is prepared to offer a substantial settlement, but they need you here to sign the papers."

"What kind of settlement?"

"Enough to make all of this go away. Enough to set you up for life if you're smart about it."

Beside her, Brandi was frowning, clearly able to hear Brandon's side of the conversation.

"I need details," Tasha said. "What exactly are they alleging? What evidence do they have?"

"Look, the specifics don't matter. What matters is that we can make this disappear if you just come back and play ball."

"The specifics absolutely matter, Brandon. If there are legitimate questions about Dante Williams' care—"

"There aren't. It's just lawyers fishing for a payday. But fighting it will cost more than settling, and it'll drag your name through the mud in the process."

Something in his tone didn't ring true. "I need time to think about it."

"There isn't time. The offer expires Monday. After that, you're on your own."

The line went dead, leaving Tasha staring at her phone.

"Well?" Brandi asked.

"I think you might be right about his motives."

"Because he's rushing you into a decision? Because he won't give you straight answers about what's actually happening?"

"All of the above." Tasha tucked her phone away, her mind clearer than it had been all morning. "I think I need to call a lawyer of my own."

"Now you're talking. And in the meantime?"

"In the meantime, I think I owe a certain veterinarian an explanation. And maybe an apology for the way I've been spiraling all morning."

Brandi grinned. "That's the Tasha I know. Ready to fight for what matters instead of running away from it."

As they walked back toward the clinic, Tasha felt something shift inside her. The fear was still there, but it was no longer paralyzing. She had decisions to make and problems to solve, but for the first time in months, she felt capable of handling them.

And she wasn't going to let Brandon or anyone else scare her away from the life she was building in Sweetgum Meadows. Especially not when that life included a man who made her remember what it felt like to hope.

Grayson had been in a good mood all morning, humming as he made his rounds and catching himself smiling for no particular reason. The memory of Tasha's kiss lingered like warmth in his chest, and he found himself looking forward to seeing her again with an anticipation that surprised him with its intensity.

He was checking on a horse with a minor leg injury at the Morrison farm when his phone rang. Tasha's name on the caller ID made his heart skip.

"Hey," he answered, unable to keep the pleasure out of his voice.

"Hi." Her voice sounded different—strained, uncertain. "Are you busy? I was wondering if we could talk."

Something in her tone immediately put him on alert. "I'm just finishing up a call. Everything okay?"

"I just... there are some things I need to explain. About last night, about my situation here."

His stomach dropped. He'd heard that tone before, usually right before someone delivered news he didn't want to hear. "Where do you want to meet?"

"Could you come by the clinic when you're done? Dr. Leighton's at lunch, so we'd have some privacy."

"I'll be there in twenty minutes."

The drive back to town felt longer than usual, his mind racing through possibilities. Had he moved too fast last night? Misread the signals? Or was this about something else entirely—the mysterious past she'd hinted at, the reason she'd left Atlanta?

By the time he parked outside the clinic, Grayson had worked himself into a state of quiet dread. He found Tasha in one of the examination rooms, standing by the window with her arms crossed, tension radiating from every line of her body.

"Thanks for coming," she said without turning around.

"Tasha, what's wrong?"

She finally faced him, and he could see the conflict in her eyes—fear warring with something that looked like determination. "I need to tell you some things about why I left Atlanta. About what I'm dealing with. And after I do, you might decide you don't want to get involved with someone who comes with so much baggage."

Grayson settled into the chair beside the examination table, giving her space but keeping his attention focused entirely on her. "I'm listening."

She took a shaky breath. "I was working in the ER at Emory University Hospital. It's a level-one trauma center, which means we got the worst cases—car accidents, shootings, overdoses. I'd been there for three years, and I was good at my job. Really good."

The pride in her voice was tinged with pain, and Grayson found himself leaning forward, wanting to offer comfort but sensing she needed to get through this without interruption.

"There was a night last October. I'd been on shift for thirty-six hours because we were short-staffed and there'd been a multi-car accident that brought in multiple critical patients. I was exhausted, running on nothing but caffeine and stubborn determination to prove I could handle whatever the department threw at me."

She paused, staring at her hands. "Dante Williams, seventeen years old, brought in after a car accident on a rainy Tuesday night. Multiple trauma, possible internal bleeding, the kind of case that should have been routine for someone with my training."

Her voice grew quieter. "The presentation was textbook at first glance—stable vitals, no obvious signs of internal injury, alert and oriented. I ordered the standard workup and moved on to the next patient, then the next. It wasn't until his blood pressure started dropping that I realized what I'd missed. By then, it was too late."

The words hung in the air between them, heavy with grief and guilt. Grayson felt his chest tighten, not with judgment but with sympathy for the weight she'd been carrying.

"There was an investigation, of course. The hospital review board, the state medical board. They all concluded that given the circumstances—my exhaustion, the chaos of that night, the subtle nature of the initial presentation—no reasonable person could have acted differently. The death was ruled unavoidable."

"But you don't believe that."

She looked up at him with surprise. "How did you—?"

"Because I know what it's like to lose someone on your watch. And I know how easy it is to blame yourself, even when everyone else says it wasn't your fault."

Something in her expression shifted, a flicker of recognition. "You've been there."

"Different circumstances, but yeah. I've been there." He thought of the soldier who'd died in his arms on a dusty road outside Baghdad, the young man whose injuries had been too severe for field medicine but whose eyes had pleaded with

Grayson to save him anyway. "Survivor's guilt is a hell of a thing."

Tasha nodded, tears threatening at the corners of her eyes. "I couldn't function after that. Couldn't trust my judgment, couldn't walk into an ER without seeing Dante Williams' face. So I took a leave of absence, tried to figure out how to put my life back together."

"And that's when you came here."

"Not immediately. I spent months in therapy, trying to process what happened. My fiancé—ex-fiancé now—was supportive at first, but eventually he got tired of my 'wallowing,' as he put it. He wanted me to go back to work, act like nothing had happened, move on."

Grayson felt a surge of anger at the unknown man who'd failed to support Tasha when she needed it most. "So you ended the engagement."

"Among other things. Brandon and I... we weren't right for each other. I was just too scared to admit it until everything fell apart." She moved away from the window, pacing to the other side of the small room. "When Dr. Leighton offered me this position, it felt like a chance to start over. Somewhere no one knew about Dante Williams or my breakdown or any of it."

"But it followed you anyway."

Her laugh was bitter. "Brandon's been calling all week. He says Dante's family is raising new questions about his care, that there might be legal action. He wants me to come back to Atlanta to help with damage control."

"Do you believe him?"

The question seemed to surprise her. "What do you mean?"

"I mean, do you trust his motives? Because from what you've told me, he doesn't sound like someone who has your best interests at heart."

Tasha was quiet for a long moment, considering. "No," she

said finally. "I don't think I trust him. The way he's handling this, pressuring me to come back immediately, offering settlements before I even know what's being alleged... it feels manipulative."

"What does your gut tell you about the case itself?"

"That I did everything I could with the information I had. That Dante Williams died because sometimes, despite our best efforts, we can't save everyone." She looked at him directly. "But knowing that intellectually and believing it emotionally are two different things."

Grayson stood, closing the distance between them. "Tasha, can I ask you something?"

She nodded.

"If one of your colleagues had been in your exact situation that night—thirty-six hours on shift, multiple trauma cases, a patient with subtle symptoms that deteriorated rapidly—what would you tell them?"

"That it wasn't their fault. That they did their best under impossible circumstances."

"But you can't extend that same compassion to yourself."

Her breath hitched. "It's different when it's your patient. Your responsibility."

"Is it?" He reached out, gently taking her hands in his. "Tasha, I've seen you work. I've seen how you handle emergencies, how you treat people. You're a good doctor. Whatever happened in Atlanta doesn't change that."

Tears spilled over then, and she leaned into him as if she couldn't hold herself up anymore. Grayson wrapped his arms around her, feeling the tremor in her shoulders as months of suppressed grief finally found release.

"I'm so tired of carrying this," she whispered against his chest.

"Then don't. Not alone, anyway."

They stood like that for several minutes, holding each other in the quiet of the examination room. Finally, Tasha pulled back, wiping her eyes with the tissues he handed her.

"So now you know," she said. "I'm a doctor who's afraid to practice medicine, running away from legal troubles that may or may not exist, with an ex-fiancé who may be trying to manipulate me into coming back to a life I don't want."

"Is that really how you see yourself?"

"Isn't it accurate?"

Grayson shook his head. "I see a doctor who cared so deeply about her patients that losing one nearly broke her. I see someone brave enough to start over in a new place, to risk opening her heart again despite everything she's been through."

"Grayson—"

"I'm not finished." His voice was gentle but firm. "I see someone who jumped in to help deliver a calf in the middle of a storm, who's already become an integral part of this community in just a few months. I see a woman I'm falling for, and I don't care what baggage you think you're carrying."

She stared at him, searching his face as if looking for signs that he didn't mean it. "You don't know what you're saying. If there is legal action, if this becomes public—"

"Then we'll deal with it. Together, if you'll let me."

"Why?" The question came out as barely a whisper. "Why would you want to take that on?"

"Because last night, for the first time in four years, I remembered what it felt like to hope for something. Because when I kissed you, I felt like I was coming back to life." He cupped her face in his hands, thumbs brushing away the remaining tears. "Because I think you're worth fighting for, even if you don't see it yet."

She closed her eyes, leaning into his touch. "I'm scared, Grayson. Scared of dragging you into my mess, scared of getting hurt again, scared of hurting you."

"Fear's not a good enough reason to walk away from something real."

"How do you know it's real? We've known each other less than a week."

"How did you know to help with Stormy's delivery? How did you know you belonged at that book club meeting? Sometimes you just know." He pressed his forehead against hers. "But I'm not asking you to decide anything right now. I'm just asking you not to run away. Not yet."

She opened her eyes, meeting his gaze. "Dr. Leighton offered me a permanent position today."

"That's good news."

"Is it? What if Brandon's right and I need to go back to Atlanta? What if staying here just makes everything worse?"

"What if it makes everything better?"

Before she could respond, the clinic door chimed, signaling Dr. Leighton's return from lunch. They stepped apart, and Tasha quickly composed herself, smoothing her hair and straightening her clothes.

"We should talk more about this," Grayson said quietly. "Tonight, maybe? I could cook dinner."

"You cook?"

"I'm full of surprises." He smiled, relieved to see her lips curve upward in response. "Seven o'clock? I'll give you directions to my place."

She nodded. "Grayson? Thank you. For listening, for not running away when I told you about Dante."

"Thank you for trusting me with it."

As he left the clinic, Grayson felt the weight of what Tasha had shared, but also a fierce protectiveness that surprised him with its intensity. She'd been carrying this burden alone for months, blaming herself for a tragedy that sounded like it could have happened to any doctor under similar circumstances.

He thought about his own journey back from the darkness

that had consumed him after Leslie's death, the slow process of learning to forgive himself for surviving when she couldn't. It had taken time and patience and the gentle insistence of people who refused to let him give up on himself.

Maybe it was time to pay that forward.

His phone buzzed with a text from Earl: "Heard you had a good evening last night. About time you started living again."

Grayson smiled, typing back: "Working on it."

And for the first time since Leslie's death, he meant it completely.

CHAPTER NINE

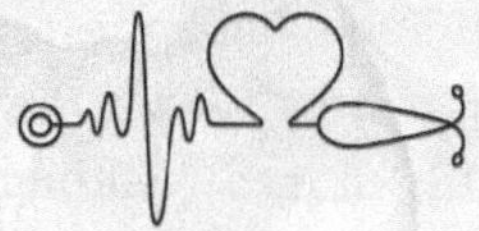

Grayson's house sat on five acres outside Sweetgum Meadows, a modest two-story farmhouse with a wraparound porch and flower boxes that showed signs of careful tending. As Tasha pulled into the gravel driveway, she could see him through the kitchen window, moving around what appeared to be a well-organized space.

She sat in her car for a moment, gathering her courage. This afternoon's conversation at the clinic had stripped away her carefully constructed walls, leaving her feeling raw and vulnerable. But also, surprisingly, lighter. For the first time in months, someone knew the truth about Dante Williams and hadn't run away.

The front door opened before she could knock, and Grayson appeared with a dish towel slung over his shoulder and flour dusting his dark shirt.

"You made it," he said, his smile warm and welcoming. "Fair warning—I may have been overly ambitious with the menu."

"It smells incredible," Tasha said, stepping into the house. The aroma of herbs and something savory filled the air, along with the faint scent of bread baking. "What are you making?"

"Chicken and dumplings, cornbread, and green beans from my own garden." He looked slightly embarrassed. "My grandmother's recipes. I thought you might like some comfort food."

The thoughtfulness of it made her chest tight. "That sounds perfect."

He led her through a living room that was clearly lived-in but tidy, with worn leather furniture and bookshelves lined with veterinary journals and what appeared to be a collection of mystery novels. Family photos sat on the mantel—Grayson in military fatigues with his unit, a wedding photo of a younger Grayson with a beautiful woman who must have been Leslie, pictures of what looked like siblings and parents.

"Your family?" Tasha asked, pausing at the mantel.

"My sister lives in Nashville with her husband and kids. My parents are in Memphis." His voice softened when he pointed to the wedding photo. "That's Leslie. We were married for six years."

"She was beautiful," Tasha said gently. "You both look so happy."

"We were. Different kind of happiness than I thought I'd ever feel again, but..." He met her eyes. "I'm learning there might be different kinds, not better or worse."

The kitchen was clearly the heart of the house, with well-worn wooden counters, copper pots hanging from hooks, and herbs growing in small pots on the windowsill. A large pot simmered on the stove, and the oven timer showed fifteen minutes remaining.

"Can I help with anything?" Tasha asked.

"Just keep me company. Tea?" He gestured to an pitcher of tea on the counter.

"Please."

As he poured two glasses, Tasha studied his profile. There was something different about him here in his own space—more relaxed, more open. The careful reserve she'd noticed in town had melted away, revealing someone who moved through his kitchen with confident familiarity.

"So," she said, accepting the glass, "you cook."

"Leslie taught me. She said if I was going to eat her cooking, I better learn to contribute." His smile held fondness rather than sadness. "Turns out I actually enjoy it. There's something soothing about following a recipe, measuring ingredients. Everything has a purpose and a place."

"Very different from emergency medicine."

"Or emergency veterinary work." He stirred the pot on the stove, then turned to face her. "How are you feeling? About this afternoon, I mean."

Tasha considered the question seriously. "Scared, still. But also relieved, I think. I've been carrying all of this alone for so long that I'd forgotten what it felt like to share the weight with someone."

"And now?"

"Now I'm wondering if I've been making everything harder than it needs to be. Brandon's been calling for weeks, making everything sound urgent and dire. But when Brandi asked me some pointed questions today, I realized I don't actually know what's happening. I've been reacting to his panic instead of getting facts."

Grayson nodded approvingly. "What's your next step?"

"I'm going to call a lawyer tomorrow. Not the hospital's lawyer, not Brandon's recommendations. My own attorney who can give me honest advice about whatever's actually going on."

"That sounds smart."

The oven timer chimed, and Grayson pulled out a pan of golden cornbread that made Tasha's mouth water. "Almost ready. Want to sit on the porch while we wait? It's a nice evening."

They settled on the porch swing with their tea, the evening air warm and filled with the sounds of crickets and distant cattle. The view stretched across rolling pasture land dotted with oak trees, peaceful in a way that made Tasha's shoulders relax.

"It's beautiful here," she said. "How did you find this place?"

"Leslie and I were looking for somewhere to start over after I got back from Iraq. Somewhere quiet where I could heal." He was quiet for a moment. "She found this house in a real estate listing, said it looked like home. She was right."

"Was it hard? Coming back?"

Grayson's jaw tightened slightly. "Harder than I expected. I thought I'd be fine—I'd been a medic, I'd saved lives. But war..." He shook his head. "War changes you in ways you don't realize until you try to go back to normal life."

"Is that why you switched from human medicine to veterinary work?"

"Partly. People ask too many questions, want to know your story. Animals just need you to show up and do your job." He glanced at her. "Though lately I'm remembering there are benefits to human connection too."

The warmth in his voice made her stomach flutter. "What kind of benefits?"

"Well, animals are terrible conversationalists. And they don't appreciate good tea."

Tasha laughed, some of the tension she'd been carrying all day finally beginning to ease. "Fair points."

They talked as the sun set, sharing stories about their training, their families, the paths that had led them both to this small town. Grayson told her about his struggles with PTSD, the nightmares that had plagued him for years, the way Leslie had patiently helped him rebuild his confidence in his own judgment.

"She sounds like an amazing woman," Tasha said.

"She was. But she's gone, and I spent four years thinking that meant I was supposed to be alone forever." He turned to look at her directly. "I don't think that anymore."

The intensity in his voice made her breath catch. "Grayson..."

"I know it's fast. I know we barely know each other. But I also know that when I'm with you, I feel like myself again. Not the broken version of myself I've been carrying around, but the person I was before everything went wrong."

Before she could respond, he stood and held out his hand. "Come on. Dinner's ready."

The meal was everything he'd promised—tender chicken and fluffy dumplings in rich broth, cornbread that was somehow both sweet and savory, green beans that tasted like they'd been picked that morning. They ate by candlelight at his small kitchen table, the conversation flowing as easily as the tea.

"This is incredible," Tasha said, savoring another bite of the dumplings. "Your grandmother must have been an amazing cook."

"She was. She lived with us when I was growing up, taught me that food was about more than nutrition. It was about taking care of people, showing them they mattered."

"Is that what you're doing now? Taking care of me?"

The question came out more vulnerable than she'd intended, but Grayson didn't seem fazed by it.

"Maybe. Is that okay?"

"I'm not used to it," she admitted. "Being taken care of, I mean. I've always been the one doing the taking care of."

"What about with Brandon?"

Tasha considered the question, twirling her fork through the dumpling broth. "With Brandon, I felt like I was always performing. Being the successful doctor, the perfect fiancée, the person who never needed help with anything."

"That sounds exhausting."

"It was. But it was also safe, in a way. If you never let anyone see your vulnerabilities, they can't use them against you."

"And now?"

She met his eyes across the table. "Now I'm sitting in your kitchen, having told you about the worst thing that's ever happened to me, and instead of running away, you cooked me dinner."

"Maybe I'm just a glutton for complicated women."

The teasing tone made her smile. "Am I complicated?"

"Incredibly. But I'm discovering I like complicated."

After dinner, they moved to the living room, where Grayson built a fire in the stone fireplace. Tasha curled up on one end of the couch, watching him work with easy competence.

"Can I ask you something?" she said when he settled beside her.

"Anything."

"Why did you really ask me to dinner tonight? Not just dinner, but here, in your home. This feels..."

"Intimate," he finished when she struggled for the word.

"Yes."

Grayson was quiet for a moment, staring into the flames. "Because when you told me about Dante Williams today, I recognized something in your voice. The way you blamed yourself, the way you've been carrying that guilt—I've been there. After Leslie died, after some of the things I saw in Iraq, I spent years thinking I was broken beyond repair."

"How did you get past it?"

"Time. Therapy. And people who refused to let me disappear into my own guilt." He turned to face her. "You're not broken, Tasha. You're hurt, and you're scared, but you're not broken."

The conviction in his voice made her eyes prick with tears. "How can you be so sure?"

"Because broken people don't jump in to help deliver calves in the middle of storms. They don't join book clubs and emergency response teams. They don't open their hearts to new possibilities."

"Is that what I'm doing? Opening my heart?"

Instead of answering with words, Grayson reached out and traced the line of her jaw with gentle fingers. "I hope so," he said quietly. "Because mine's been closed for four years, and you're the first person who's made me want to open it again."

When he kissed her this time, it was different from their first kiss on her doorstep. Deeper, more certain, with an undercurrent of promise that made her head spin. She found herself melting against him, her hands fisting in his shirt as four months of loneliness and fear gave way to something warm and bright and hopeful.

"Stay," he whispered against her lips when they broke apart, both breathing hard.

The word hung between them, loaded with possibility and risk. Tasha felt her heart racing, torn between the desire to lose herself in his warmth and the voice in her head that insisted she was moving too fast, getting in too deep.

"Grayson, I don't know if I'm ready—"

"Not for that," he said quickly, understanding her hesitation. "Just stay. Talk to me, I have two spare bedrooms that you can choose from, let me make you breakfast in the morning. I'm not trying to rush you into anything you're not ready for."

The gentleness in his voice, the way he seemed to understand exactly what she needed without her having to explain it, made something in her chest crack open.

"Okay," she said softly. "I'll stay."

They talked until nearly midnight, sharing stories and secrets by the dying fire. Grayson talked about his time in the military, the bonds formed with fellow soldiers, the way coming home had felt like landing on an alien planet.

When her eyelids grew heavy, he guided her to one of the guestrooms.

"Is this room okay, or would you like the other?" he asked.

"This is perfect," she said, and meant it. The room was cozy and had an old-time charm.

He kissed her forehead softly. "Sleep well. I'll be down the hall in my room if you need anything."

After he left, Tasha lay in the darkness, listening to the house settle around her. For the first time in months, the anxiety that usually kept her awake was quiet. In its place was something she'd almost forgotten how to recognize: peace.

Her phone buzzed with a text from Brandon: "Deadline is Monday. After that, you're on your own."

Instead of the usual panic, she felt only a mild irritation. Tomorrow she would call a lawyer. Tomorrow she would get real answers about what was happening with Dante Williams' case. Tomorrow she would start taking control of her life instead of letting fear make her decisions.

But tonight, she was in Grayson's house, surrounded by the lingering scents of dinner and the sound of him moving around upstairs. Tonight, she was exactly where she wanted to be.

She turned off her phone and pulled the blanket up to her chin, smiling as she drifted off to sleep. For the first time since leaving Atlanta, Tasha felt like she might actually have found her way home.

CHAPTER TEN

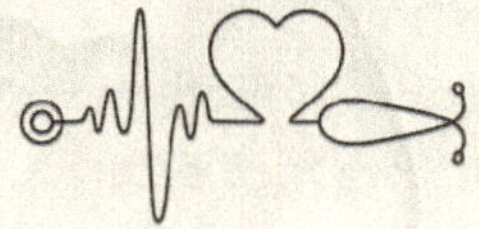

Grayson woke to the smell of coffee brewing and the sound of quiet movement downstairs. For a moment, he lay still, absorbing the unfamiliar pleasure of knowing someone else was in his house—not just anyone, but Tasha, who had trusted him enough to stay the night even when her instincts probably told her to run.

He found her in the kitchen, dressed in yesterday's clothes but somehow looking perfectly at home as she moved around his space. She'd found the coffee filters and figured out his machine, and was now studying the contents of his refrigerator with the focused attention of someone planning breakfast.

"Morning," he said, padding barefoot across the tile floor.

She turned with a smile that made his chest warm. "I hope you don't mind. I'm an early riser, and I thought I'd return the favor from last night."

"What did you have in mind?"

"Scrambled eggs, if you have them. Maybe some of that bread toasted." She gestured to the loaf of homemade bread his neighbor Mrs. Patterson had brought by earlier in the week.

"I'm not as ambitious a cook as you are, but I can manage breakfast."

"Sounds perfect." He moved to the cabinet and pulled down plates, hyperaware of her presence in his kitchen. There was something deeply satisfying about this domestic scene—the two of them moving around each other with easy familiarity, sharing space and simple tasks.

As she cracked eggs into a bowl, Tasha glanced at him. "I called a lawyer this morning. Found one in the next county who specializes in medical malpractice defense."

"That was fast."

"I figured there was no point in putting it off. His secretary said he could see me this afternoon if I drove over." She whisked the eggs with more force than necessary. "I'm nervous about what I might find out."

Grayson moved behind her, resting his hands lightly on her shoulders. "Whatever it is, you'll handle it. And you won't be handling it alone."

She leaned back against him briefly. "I keep waiting for you to come to your senses and realize you don't want to get involved in this mess."

"Not going to happen."

"How can you be so sure?"

He turned her around to face him, noting the vulnerability in her eyes despite the determined set of her jaw. "Because I've spent four years playing it safe, keeping everyone at arm's length to avoid getting hurt again. And I'm tired of being safe. I'm tired of being alone."

"Even if being with me means dealing with lawyers and potential lawsuits and—"

He silenced her with a gentle kiss. "Even then."

They ate breakfast on the back porch, watching the morning mist rise from the pastures. Grayson found himself studying

Tasha's profile as she sipped her coffee, noting the way the early light caught in her hair and the gradual relaxation in her posture as the caffeine kicked in.

"What's your day looking like?" she asked.

"Two farm calls this morning, then office hours this afternoon. Should be done by four." He hesitated, then added, "I could drive over with you to meet with the lawyer, if you want the moral support."

Tasha's expression softened. "You'd do that?"

"If you want me there."

She reached across the small table and took his hand. "I'd like that. I'd like it a lot."

The drive to Millbrook took them through countryside that was becoming familiar—rolling hills, cattle grazing in morning pastures, farmhouses with wide porches and carefully tended gardens. Tasha was quiet for most of the trip, her fingers drumming nervously against her thigh as she stared out the window.

"Talk to me," Grayson said when they were about ten minutes from town. "What's going through your head?"

"I keep thinking about Dante Williams' parents. About how they trusted me to save their son, and I failed them." Her voice was barely above a whisper. "What if Brandon's right? What if there really are questions about my care that night?"

"Then you'll answer them. With facts, with the truth about what happened."

"What if the truth isn't good enough?"

Grayson pulled into the parking lot of the law office and turned off the engine. "Tasha, look at me."

She met his eyes, and he could see the fear there, the self-doubt that had been eating at her for months.

"You're a good doctor. I've seen you work, remember? You're competent and caring and exactly the kind of person I'd want treating someone I loved." He reached over and cupped her face gently. "Whatever happened that night, it wasn't because you didn't care enough or try hard enough. Sometimes people die despite our best efforts. That's not your fault."

Her eyes filled with tears. "I just want to know for sure. One way or the other."

"Then let's go find out."

The law office of Michael Harrison, Esq. was located in a converted Victorian house with creaky floors and the kind of worn furniture that suggested practicality over pretension. Harrison himself was a man in his sixties with gray hair and kind eyes behind wire-rimmed glasses.

"Dr. Jenkins," he said, rising from behind a desk covered in case files. "Thank you for coming in. I understand you have some questions about a case in Atlanta?"

Tasha settled into the chair across from his desk, her hands clasped tightly in her lap. "I'm not even sure there is a case. My ex-fiancé has been calling, claiming the family of a patient who died is raising questions, but he won't give me specifics."

"Tell me about the patient."

Grayson listened as Tasha recounted the events of that October night—the thirty-six hour shift, the multiple trauma cases, Dante Williams' initial presentation and rapid deterioration. Her voice was steady as she described the medical details, but he could see the pain in her eyes as she relived those final moments.

"And the official investigation?" Harrison asked, making notes as she spoke.

"Hospital review board found no negligence. State medical board reached the same conclusion. The death was ruled unavoidable given the circumstances."

Harrison nodded. "Do you have copies of those reports?"

"In my apartment back in Sweetgum Meadows."

"I'd like to review them, along with the medical records from that night." He leaned back in his chair, studying her face. "Dr. Jenkins, based on what you've told me, this sounds like a tragic case but not necessarily one with legal merit. The fact that two separate review boards found no negligence is significant."

"But Brandon said—"

"What exactly did he say? His precise words?"

Tasha frowned, clearly trying to remember. "That the family was asking questions about the care Dante received. That there might be legal action. That the hospital wanted to offer a settlement to make it go away."

"Did he mention any specific attorney representing the family? Any filed paperwork? Formal complaints to the medical board?"

"No. He just kept saying it was urgent, that I needed to come back to Atlanta immediately."

Harrison exchanged a look with Grayson that suggested he was thinking the same thing—that Brandon's urgency didn't quite add up.

"Dr. Jenkins, would you mind if I made some calls? I have contacts in Atlanta who can check whether any formal action has actually been filed. It should take me a day or two to get answers."

"You can do that?"

"It's all public record once formal proceedings begin. And if nothing's been filed..." He shrugged. "Then your ex-fiancé may be manufacturing a crisis that doesn't exist."

The drive back to Sweetgum Meadows was quieter, but Tasha's tension had eased considerably. "I feel like an idiot," she said as they crossed the county line. "All these weeks of panic, and there might not even be anything to panic about."

"You're not an idiot. You're someone who's been manipulated by a person you trusted."

"Why would Brandon do that? What does he gain by getting me back to Atlanta?"

Grayson had some theories about that, none of them charitable toward her ex-fiancé, but he kept them to himself. "Maybe he misses you. Maybe he thinks if he can get you back there, you'll stay."

"That's not going to happen." The certainty in her voice was reassuring. "Whatever my reasons for leaving Atlanta were originally, I've found something here that I don't want to give up."

"What's that?"

She turned to look at him, her expression soft but determined. "A life that feels like mine. Work that matters, friends who care about me as a person rather than just my professional achievements. And..."

"And?"

"And you. I don't want to give up you."

The simple statement hit him harder than any declaration of love could have. This wasn't about grand passion or overwhelming emotion—it was about choice, about Tasha actively deciding that what they were building together was worth fighting for.

"You won't have to," he said quietly. "I'm not going anywhere."

They stopped by Tasha's apartment so she could change clothes and gather the documentation Harrison had requested. While she was upstairs, Grayson waited in his truck, thinking about the morning's revelations.

If Harrison was right and there was no actual legal action pending, then Brandon had been pressuring Tasha to return to Atlanta under false pretenses. The question was whether he'd been genuinely mistaken about the threat or deliberately lying to manipulate her.

Either way, Grayson felt a fierce protectiveness toward the woman who'd trusted him with her fears and vulnerabilities. Tasha had spent months blaming herself for a tragedy that sounded increasingly like it couldn't have been prevented. She didn't need the added stress of dealing with an ex-fiancé who couldn't accept that their relationship was over.

She emerged from the building with a manila folder under her arm and a lighter expression than he'd seen in days.

"Got everything," she said, sliding into the passenger seat. "I also called Dr. Leighton and told him I'm ready to discuss that permanent position."

"Yeah?"

"Yeah. Whatever happens with Atlanta, I want to stay here. I want to build a life in Sweetgum Meadows."

"What changed your mind?"

She reached over and took his hand, intertwining their fingers. "Realizing that running away from problems doesn't actually solve them. And realizing that I've found something here worth staying for."

The afternoon passed quickly. Grayson completed his scheduled appointments while Tasha returned to the clinic for her regular shift. They met up for dinner at Rochelle's Old-Fashioned Diner, where Malakai insisted on preparing something special "for the town's new favorite couple."

"Word travels fast," Tasha observed as they settled into a booth near the window.

"Small town living," Grayson agreed. "Everyone knows everyone's business."

"Do you mind? People talking about us?"

He considered the question seriously. "Six months ago, I would have minded. I liked my privacy, liked being able to disappear into my work without people speculating about my personal life."

"And now?"

"Now I'm discovering there are advantages to being part of a community. People care about what happens to you. They want you to be happy."

As if to prove his point, Malakai appeared with their meals

and a knowing smile. "On the house tonight," he said, waving away Grayson's attempt to pay. "Consider it a celebration."

"What are we celebrating?" Tasha asked.

"Dr. Leighton stopped by earlier. Mentioned you'd accepted his offer to stay on permanently. That's good news for all of us."

After Malakai left, Tasha shook her head in amazement. "In Atlanta, I could work with people for years and they'd never know my personal business. Here, I make one phone call and the whole town knows about it by dinner."

"Having second thoughts?"

"About staying? No. About privacy? Maybe a little." She smiled. "But I'm learning there are worse things than having people care about your happiness."

They were finishing their meal when Tasha's phone rang. Harrison's name appeared on the screen, and she answered immediately.

"Mr. Harrison? Do you have news?"

Grayson watched her face as she listened to the lawyer's response, noting the way her shoulders straightened and her expression cleared.

"I see. Yes, I understand. Thank you so much for checking."

She ended the call and looked at Grayson with something approaching relief.

"Well?"

"No formal action has been filed. No complaints to the medical board. No attorney representing the Williams family has contacted anyone at the hospital."

"So Brandon was lying."

"Or at least seriously exaggerating." She set down her phone with a decisive gesture. "Harrison thinks I should document the harassment—all the phone calls, the pressure tactics, the threats about deadlines that apparently don't exist."

"In case you need a restraining order?"

"In case he escalates. Apparently this kind of behavior isn't uncommon in contentious breakups, especially when there's professional success or financial security involved."

Grayson felt anger flare at the thought of Brandon manipulating Tasha's grief and guilt for his own purposes. "What's your next step?"

"Harrison's going to send a cease and desist letter. Formal notice that I don't want any further contact unless it's through an attorney regarding legitimate legal matters."

"And if he ignores it?"

"Then we escalate. But hopefully it won't come to that." She reached across the table and took his hand. "I can't believe I let him manipulate me for so long. All those sleepless nights, all that anxiety about something that wasn't even real."

"You were grieving and guilty and trying to process a traumatic experience. He took advantage of that."

"Still, I should have been smarter."

"You were human. There's a difference."

As they walked back to their cars, Tasha stopped suddenly and turned to face him. "Thank you."

"For what?"

"For not letting me run away. For insisting I get real answers instead of accepting Brandon's version of events. For believing in me when I couldn't believe in myself."

Instead of responding with words, Grayson pulled her into his arms and kissed her, there on the sidewalk outside the diner with half the town probably watching from inside. When they broke apart, both were breathing hard.

"Does this mean we're officially the town's favorite couple?" Tasha asked, glancing toward the diner windows where several faces quickly disappeared from view.

"Looks that way. You okay with that?"

She considered the question seriously, then smiled. "You know what? I really am."

As Grayson drove home that night, he reflected on how

much had changed in just a few days. Tasha was staying in Sweetgum Meadows. The legal cloud hanging over her was lifting. And for the first time since Leslie's death, he was building something real with someone who mattered.

It felt like stepping back into the light after years of shadows. And he was ready for whatever came next.

CHAPTER ELEVEN

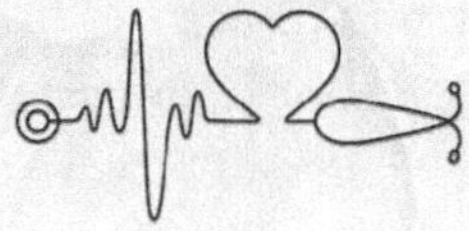

Three weeks had passed since the meeting with Harrison, and Tasha was finally beginning to feel like she could breathe again. The cease and desist letter had worked —Brandon's calls had stopped completely, leaving behind a silence that felt more like peace than abandonment. Her work at Dr. Leighton's clinic was everything she'd hoped for: challenging cases, grateful patients, and the growing sense that she was exactly where she belonged.

This morning, she was reviewing charts when Margaret, the receptionist, knocked on her office door.

"Dr. Jenkins? There's someone here to see you. Says it's personal."

Tasha's stomach immediately clenched. Her first thought was that Brandon had decided to ignore the lawyer's letter and show up in person. But when she walked to the front desk, she found a woman about her own age with kind eyes and graying hair pulled back in a neat bun.

"Dr. Jenkins? I'm Patricia Williams. I was wondering if we could talk."

The name hit Tasha like a physical blow. Williams. Dante's mother.

"Of course," Tasha managed, her mouth suddenly dry. "Would you like to step into my office?"

Patricia Williams was smaller than Tasha had imagined, with the careful composure of someone who had learned to carry grief without letting it consume her. She settled into the chair across from Tasha's desk and folded her hands in her lap.

"I know this must be a shock," Patricia said quietly. "I probably should have called first, but I wasn't sure you'd agree to see me."

"How did you find me?" Tasha asked, then immediately regretted the question. It sounded defensive, almost accusatory.

"Your former colleague, Dr. Morrison, mentioned you'd relocated to a small town in Georgia. It took some detective work to track down exactly where." Patricia's smile was sad but not unkind. "I hope you don't mind the intrusion. I just... I needed to talk to someone who was there that night."

Tasha felt her hands begin to tremble and clasped them together under her desk. "Mrs. Williams, I want you to know how deeply sorry I am about Dante. I've thought about him every day since—"

"Please," Patricia interrupted gently. "Let me go first. I need to say something, and I'm afraid if I don't get it out now, I might lose my nerve."

Tasha nodded, not trusting her voice.

"I came here to thank you."

The words were so unexpected that Tasha was sure she'd misheard. "I'm sorry?"

"To thank you," Patricia repeated. "For everything you did for my son that night. For fighting for him, for not giving up even when things looked impossible."

Tears sprang to Tasha's eyes. "Mrs. Williams, I failed him. I missed the signs of internal bleeding until it was too late. If I had been more thorough in my initial assessment—"

"Dr. Jenkins." Patricia's voice was firm but compassionate. "May I tell you what I learned during the investigation?"

Tasha could only nod.

"I learned that you had been on duty for thirty-six hours when Dante arrived. That you had already treated fourteen trauma patients that shift, including three who required emergency surgery. I learned that Dante's initial presentation was stable enough that any reasonable physician would have triaged him as they did."

Patricia reached into her purse and pulled out a thick folder. "I also learned that in your three years at Emory, you had one of the highest success rates in the emergency department. That your colleagues called you 'the doctor they'd want treating their own families.' That you had saved countless lives before that terrible night."

"But I didn't save Dante."

"No, you didn't. But not because you didn't try hard enough or care enough or know enough. You didn't save him because sometimes, despite our best efforts and all our training and technology, people die. Even young, healthy people like my son."

Tasha was crying openly now, eighteen months of guilt and self-recrimination pouring out in ugly, heaving sobs. Patricia moved around the desk and knelt beside her chair, placing a gentle hand on her shoulder.

"Honey, you have to stop blaming yourself. Dante's death was a tragedy, but it wasn't your fault. The review boards made that clear. The other doctors who examined his case made that clear. Everyone except you has accepted that truth."

"I keep thinking about what I could have done differently," Tasha whispered through her tears. "If I had ordered different tests, if I had checked on him sooner—"

"If you had been superhuman instead of human," Patricia said gently. "Dr. Jenkins, my husband and I grieved for months. We were angry and lost and looking for someone to blame. But when we really examined what happened that night, when we understood the impossible circumstances you were working under, we realized something important."

"What?"

"That you gave our son every chance he had. That you fought for him with everything you had, even when you were exhausted beyond reason. That you cared about him as more than just another case." Patricia's own eyes were bright with tears. "And that means everything to a parent."

They sat in silence for several minutes, Patricia's hand steady on Tasha's shoulder as the storm of emotion gradually subsided. Finally, Tasha lifted her head and reached for the tissues on her desk.

"I don't understand," she said, her voice hoarse. "Someone told my ex-fiancé that you were raising questions about Dante's care. That there might be legal action."

Patricia's expression darkened. "We never spoke to anyone about pursuing legal action. We never contacted the hospital with new questions. As far as I know, no one in our family has had any contact with your former colleagues since the investigation was closed."

A chill ran down Tasha's spine. "So Brandon was lying."

"I don't know who Brandon is, but if someone told him we were pursuing legal action, they were either mistaken or deliberately misleading him." Patricia returned to her chair, studying Tasha's face with concern. "Is that why you left Atlanta? Because you thought we were coming after you?"

"Partly. I was also struggling with PTSD, with my confidence in my own judgment. I couldn't function in an emergency room anymore."

"And now?"

Tasha considered the question. Over the past few weeks, she'd been taking on more complex cases at Dr. Leighton's clinic, handling situations that would have paralyzed her with fear six months ago. The old confidence wasn't fully back, but it was growing stronger each day.

"Now I'm learning to trust myself again. Slowly."

"I'm glad. The medical profession needs doctors like you—doctors who care so deeply about their patients that losing one nearly breaks them. That kind of compassion can't be taught."

They talked for another hour, Patricia sharing memories of Dante—his dreams of becoming an engineer, his love of basketball, the way he always made her laugh even on her worst days. In return, Tasha found herself describing the doctor she'd been before that October night, the passion for emergency medicine that had driven her to push herself beyond reasonable limits.

"You know," Patricia said as she prepared to leave, "Dante would have liked knowing that his doctor cared so much about him. He was always drawn to people who wore their hearts on their sleeves."

"Thank you for coming," Tasha said, meaning it completely. "I can't tell you what this means to me."

"I should have come sooner. I just didn't know how to find you, and I wasn't sure..." Patricia paused at the door. "Dr. Jenkins, I hope you'll consider returning to emergency medicine someday. Not necessarily at a big hospital, but somewhere. The world needs doctors like you."

After Patricia left, Tasha sat in her office for a long time, processing everything that had just happened. The guilt that had been her constant companion for eighteen months hadn't disappeared entirely, but it had transformed into something more manageable—grief for a young life lost, yes, but not the crushing self-blame that had driven her from Atlanta.

Her phone buzzed with a text from Grayson: "How's your day going? Still on for dinner tonight?"

She stared at the message, thinking about how to explain what had just happened. Then she typed back: "It's been a life-changing kind of day. Definitely still on for dinner. I have a lot to tell you."

The response came immediately: "Good news or bad news?"

"Good news. Really, really good news."

That evening, she found herself on Grayson's porch with a bottle of wine and a lightness in her chest that she hadn't felt in months. He took one look at her face and smiled.

"You look different," he said, pulling her into his arms for a hello kiss that made her toes curl.

"I feel different. Patricia Williams came to see me today."

Grayson's expression immediately grew serious. "Dante's mother? Here?"

"She came to thank me." The words still felt surreal. "To tell me that she and her husband never blamed me for what happened, that they understood the circumstances I was working under that night."

As they cooked dinner together—a simple pasta dish that required minimal attention—Tasha recounted the entire conversation. Grayson listened without interruption, his expression growing increasingly thoughtful.

"So Brandon was definitely lying about the legal action," he said when she finished.

"Definitely. Which means he was willing to exploit my guilt and trauma to manipulate me into coming back to Atlanta."

"Are you angry?"

Tasha considered the question as she tossed the salad. "I should be furious. But mostly I just feel... free. Like I've been carrying a weight that was never mine to carry in the first place."

They ate on the back porch as the sun set, talking about

Patricia's visit and what it meant for Tasha's future. The conversation meandered to other topics—Grayson's expanding practice, the book club's latest dramatic interpretation of a romance novel, the way their relationship had become part of Sweetgum Meadows' social fabric.

"I've been thinking," Tasha said as they shared a slice of pie. "About my work here, about what I want to do next."

"What kind of thinking?"

"Dr. Leighton mentioned that the hospital has been looking for someone to help with emergency cases—not full ER work, but the kind of urgent situations that are too complex for a family practice." She paused, watching his face. "I think I'm ready for that kind of challenge again."

"That sounds like it would be right up your alley."

"It would. And Patricia's visit today made me realize something—I'm not afraid of emergency medicine anymore. I'm ready to get back to what I love."

Grayson reached across the table and took her hand. "How does it feel to say that?"

"Scary. Exciting. Right." She squeezed his fingers. "I've spent so long running from that part of myself that I'd forgotten how much I missed it."

"What would this arrangement mean? Practically, I mean."

"I'd still work with Dr. Leighton most of the time, but I'd be on call for emergency cases at the hospital. More variety, more challenge, but not the overwhelming pace of a big city ER."

The question hung in the air between them, loaded with implications about the future they were building together. Tasha met his eyes directly.

"It would mean I'm not going anywhere. That I'm committed to building a life here, with you, for as long as you'll have me."

Instead of answering with words, Grayson stood and pulled her up into his arms, kissing her with a passion that made her forget about everything except the taste of him and the solid warmth of his body against hers.

"I love you," he whispered against her lips, the words coming out as if they'd been building pressure for weeks.

"I love you too," she whispered back, and felt something settle into place in her chest—the final piece of a puzzle she'd been working on without realizing it.

When he kissed her this time, she felt the difference in the way his hands trembled slightly as they framed her face.

"Tasha," he whispered against her lips.

"I know," she breathed back, her fingers finding the buttons of his shirt.

He caught her hands gently. "Are you sure?"

Instead of answering with words, she stood on her toes and kissed him again, deeper this time, until he made a low sound in his throat that sent heat racing through her veins.

He led her upstairs, their fingers intertwined. On the landing, she paused, touching the thin scar that ran across his chest.

"From the IED," he said quietly, watching her face.

"Does it hurt?"

"Not anymore."

She pressed her lips to the scar, felt him shudder beneath her touch.

"Tasha..."

"Show me," she whispered. "Show me what it means to come home."

THE LAMP CAST golden light across tangled sheets. Tasha traced lazy patterns on his chest while his fingers combed through her hair.

"I never thought I'd feel this again," he murmured.

"What?"

"Like all the broken pieces fit back together."

She lifted her head to study his face. "This feels different than anything I've ever experienced."

"How so?"

"Safe. Real. Like I can finally stop pretending to be someone I'm not."

His arm tightened around her. "What were you pretending to be?"

"Perfect. Unbreakable. The doctor who never made mistakes." Her voice grew quiet. "The woman who didn't need anyone."

"And now?"

"Now I know I want to be with you. And somehow that doesn't scare me anymore."

They talked until dawn crept through the windows—about her new role at the hospital, about expanding his practice, about the life they were building together.

"I should probably go back to my apartment soon," she said as sunlight painted the walls gold. "Get some clothes, check my mail."

"Or," Grayson said carefully, "you could bring your things here. If you want to."

She turned to face him fully. "Are you asking me to move in with you?"

"I'm asking if you'd want to. No pressure, but... I like having you here. I like the way your coffee mug looks next to mine in the sink."

Tasha smiled, pressing a kiss to his collarbone. "I'd like that too. Very much."

"Yeah?"

"Yeah. I think it's time to stop keeping one foot out the door."

As Tasha drifted off in his arms, she thought about the long journey that had brought her here—from the trauma of Dante Williams' death through months of guilt and self-doubt to this moment of peace and possibility. It hadn't been a straight path, and there would likely be more challenges ahead, but for the first time in eighteen months, she felt ready to face whatever came next.

She was home. She was loved. And tomorrow, she would start building a future that felt entirely her own.

CHAPTER TWELVE

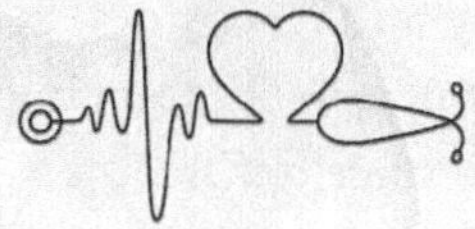

Two weeks had passed since Tasha had moved in completely, and Grayson was still discovering small pleasures in their shared life. Her medical journals mixed with his veterinary texts on the bedside table, her favorite tea beside his coffee in the kitchen cabinet, the way she hummed while getting dressed for work each morning.

This morning, he was finishing up paperwork from yesterday's calls when his phone rang. Earl's name appeared on the screen.

"Morning, Earl. What can I do for you?"

"Doc, I hate to bother you, but I've got a situation with Thunder. He's not acting right, and I'm worried."

"I'll be right there."

Grayson grabbed his emergency kit and headed for his truck. The drive to Earl's farm gave him time to think about how much his life had changed in recent months. Not just because of Tasha—though her presence had transformed everything—but because he felt more connected to the community than he had in years.

Earl's farm appeared around the bend, and Grayson could

see a cluster of people gathered near the main paddock. As he pulled up, Earl hurried over with worry etched across his weathered face.

"Doc, thanks for coming so quick. It's Thunder—he's down and won't get up. Been like this for about an hour."

Grayson grabbed his kit and followed Earl toward the paddock where a large chestnut gelding lay on his side, breathing heavily. Casey and Aria stood at the fence, Aria's face pale with worry but no longer showing the paralyzing fear around animals that had once defined her.

"What happened?" Grayson asked, kneeling beside the horse and beginning his examination.

"Found him like this when I came out to check on the herd. No obvious injuries, but he's not responding normally."

Grayson worked quickly, checking Thunder's vital signs, examining his eyes and gums, palpating his abdomen. The horse's temperature was elevated, and his breathing was labored.

"Looks like colic," he said, continuing his assessment. "I can treat him here, but I'll need to monitor him closely for the next few hours."

As Grayson worked to administer medication and fluids, Aria approached without hesitation.

"Can I help?" she asked, no trace of her former anxiety.

"You can talk to him. Let him know he's not alone. Animals respond to calm, gentle voices."

For the next hour, Aria sat by Thunder's head, stroking his neck and speaking in soft, reassuring tones while Grayson monitored his condition. It was a remarkable transformation from the frightened little girl who'd once been too scared to enter the barn.

"She's come so far," Casey said quietly, watching her daughter with obvious pride. "Six months ago, she wouldn't even pet a dog. Now she's reading veterinary textbooks online."

"She's got good instincts," Grayson replied. "And she's not afraid to care about something, even when it's vulnerable."

Gradually, Thunder's breathing improved and he began showing signs of recovery. When the horse finally struggled to his feet and walked to the water trough, Aria let out a cheer that made everyone smile.

"You did good, Thunder," she said, patting his neck with newfound confidence. "Dr. Mitchell saved you."

As Grayson packed his equipment, Earl walked him back to his truck. "Can't thank you enough, Doc. Thunder's been part of this family for eight years."

"Just glad we caught it early. He should be fine, but call me if you notice any changes."

Earl nodded, then glanced toward the house where Casey and Aria were visible through the kitchen window. "You know, that girl's got a real gift with animals now. Amazing what confidence can do."

"She just needed someone to show her it was safe."

"Speaking of confidence..." Earl's weathered face creased into a knowing smile. "You seem different these days, Doc. Happier. More settled."

Grayson felt the familiar warmth that always came when someone mentioned his relationship with Tasha. "I am. Tasha's... she's made a real difference in my life."

"Good to see. You've been on your own long enough." Earl's tone was matter-of-fact, free of pity or pressure. "The whole community's noticed how well you two fit together."

"Have they?"

"Oh yes. But in a good way—people are happy for you. It's nice when two good people find each other."

On the drive home, Grayson reflected on Earl's words. He had been aware of the community's quiet acceptance of his relationship with Tasha, but he was still getting used to being part of that social fabric rather than existing on its edges.

He stopped at the feed store to pick up supplies, and found himself in conversation with Tom Bradley, who owned the neighboring farm.

"Heard you saved Earl's horse this morning," Tom said as they loaded bags of grain into Grayson's truck. "Thunder's a good animal."

"Just doing my job."

"Still, Earl appreciates having someone he can count on." Tom secured the last bag. "And speaking of counting on people, how's Dr. Jenkins settling in? My wife mentioned she's started working with the hospital on emergency cases."

"She has. She's enjoying the challenge."

"That's good to hear. We're lucky to have another skilled doctor in the area." Tom's smile was genuine. "And it's nice seeing you with someone who obviously makes you happy."

The comment was casual, offered without expectation of response, but it struck Grayson how natural these conversations had become. People weren't prying or gossiping—they were simply acknowledging that he and Tasha were building something together, and they approved.

At the hardware store, he encountered Mrs. Patterson, who was selecting paint colors for her kitchen.

"Dr. Mitchell! How are you? And how is Dr. Jenkins?"

"We're both doing well, thank you."

"I'm so glad. You know, I had to take my grandson to the hospital last week—just a minor accident on his bicycle—and Dr. Jenkins was the one who treated him. Such a competent, caring doctor. And Tommy felt so comfortable with her."

"She has a gift for putting people at ease."

"She does indeed. And it's lovely seeing you two together at community events. You both seem so content."

These interactions continued throughout his errands—casual mentions of his and Tasha's relationship, expressions of genuine pleasure at their happiness, the kind of community recognition that came without pressure or intrusion. By the time he headed home, Grayson felt a deep appreciation for the way Sweetgum Meadows had embraced them as a couple.

Home felt especially welcoming when he arrived. Tasha was in the kitchen, still in her scrubs but with an apron tied over them, something savory bubbling on the stove. She looked up as he entered, her face lighting up with the kind of smile that still made his chest tight with affection.

"Perfect timing," she said, rising on her toes to kiss him hello. "I'm experimenting with that chicken stew recipe your grandmother used to make. I may have added a few extra vegetables."

"Smells incredible. How was your day at the hospital?"

"Busy. Good busy." She stirred the pot, her movements confident and happy. "I handled a car accident case today—multiple trauma, but nothing I couldn't manage. It felt... right. Like I was exactly where I belonged."

"That's wonderful."

"Dr. Martinez—he's the ER chief—mentioned something interesting. He said the hospital's been getting more calls for consultation on cases that involve both people and animals. Farm accidents, mostly."

Grayson raised an eyebrow. "Is that common?"

"More than you'd think. Apparently word has gotten out that I'm living with the area's best large animal vet." She grinned at him. "He asked if you might be interested in being on call for those kinds of situations."

The idea was intriguing. "That could be useful. I've been to several calls where the farmer needed medical attention too, but I'm obviously not qualified to treat humans."

"Exactly. And I've noticed that understanding animal behavior and farm operations makes me a better doctor when treating agricultural injuries."

They discussed the possibility over dinner, both excited by the prospect of occasionally working together. It felt like another natural evolution of their relationship—their skills complementing each other in ways that could benefit the entire community.

"Dr. Martinez wants to set up a meeting to discuss protocols," Tasha said as they cleaned up. "Would you be interested?"

"Definitely."

"Good. Because I already told him yes." She grinned sheepishly. "I was pretty sure you'd agree."

"You know me well."

"I'm learning."

Saturday morning brought a call from Brandi, inviting them to a community barbecue at the park. "Just a casual get-together," she explained. "But we wanted to make sure you two knew you were welcome."

"Should we go?" Tasha asked after relaying the invitation.

Grayson considered it. Six months ago, he would have politely declined, preferring the safety of his own space. Now, the idea of spending an afternoon with neighbors and friends sounded appealing.

"I think it might be nice," he said.

The park was bustling when they arrived, picnic tables laden with covered dishes and families scattered across the grass. Children ran between the trees with kites and frisbees, while adults clustered in comfortable groups, conversations flowing easily.

"Dr. Mitchell! Dr. Jenkins!" Aria came running over, her confidence around animals now extending to general enthusiasm for life. "Come see what we're doing!"

She led them to where a group of children had set up an impromptu veterinary clinic using stuffed animals as patients. "I'm teaching them how to check for injuries, like you showed me with Thunder."

Grayson watched as Aria demonstrated proper animal

handling techniques to her friends, her earlier fears completely transformed into knowledge she was eager to share.

"She's going to make an excellent veterinarian," Tasha said quietly.

"If that's what she chooses. But she'll excel at whatever she does, with that kind of confidence and compassion."

They spent the afternoon moving naturally through the crowd, included in conversations that went beyond polite pleasantries. Farmers asked for Grayson's advice on animal health issues, parents wanted Tasha's opinion on minor injuries their children had sustained, and everywhere they went, people seemed genuinely pleased to see them together.

"You know what I love about this?" Tasha said as they sat on a picnic blanket, watching children chase fireflies in the gathering dusk.

"What?"

"Nobody's treating us like we're still figuring things out. They're treating us like we belong together. Like we're already family."

She was right. At some point during the past few weeks, the community had quietly accepted them as a unit. Invitations came addressed to both of them, people asked about their plans as a couple, and their relationship had become part of the town's social fabric without fanfare or pressure.

"Is that what we are?" Grayson asked. "Family?"

Tasha turned to look at him, her expression soft but certain. "I think we are. Don't you?"

Instead of answering with words, he leaned over and kissed her, there in the middle of the community gathering with half of Sweetgum Meadows as witnesses. When they broke apart, a few people nearby had noticed and were smiling approvingly, but no one made a fuss or called attention to the moment.

It was perfect in its simplicity—a kiss between two people

who belonged together, witnessed by a community that cared about their happiness.

As they helped clean up after the barbecue, Mrs. Bridges approached with a warm smile.

"Lovely afternoon," she said. "So nice to see the whole community come together like this."

"It really was," Tasha agreed. "Thank you for making sure we knew about it."

"Oh honey, you're part of this community now. Of course you'd be included." Mrs. Bridges's smile was maternal and fond. "It does my heart good to see two people who've found their place in the world, both individually and together."

Later that evening, as they sat on their back porch with glasses of wine, Grayson reflected on the day's events.

"I never expected this," Tasha said, echoing his thoughts.

"What?"

"To feel so settled so quickly. To be part of something larger than just us." She leaned against his shoulder. "I spent so many years feeling like I was performing my life instead of living it. This feels like living it."

Grayson understood exactly what she meant. For years after Leslie's death, he'd gone through the motions of existence without truly engaging with the world around him. Now, with Tasha beside him and the community's warm acceptance surrounding them both, he felt fully present in his own life again.

"I love our life," Tasha said quietly.

"Me too."

And for the first time in years, that simple statement felt like the complete truth.

CHAPTER THIRTEEN

The emergency call came in just as Tasha was finishing her morning rounds at Dr. Leighton's clinic. Margaret burst through the office door, her usual calm demeanor replaced by urgent efficiency.

"Dr. Jenkins, we've got a situation at the Hendricks farm. Multiple injuries—both human and animal. The hospital's requesting you respond, and they've already called Dr. Mitchell."

Tasha's pulse immediately quickened, not with the old panic that used to accompany emergency calls, but with the familiar rush of adrenaline that meant her skills were needed. "What's the situation?"

"Farm equipment accident. Mr. Hendricks got caught under an overturned tractor, and there are injured cattle at the scene. Paramedics are en route, but they need medical support on-site."

"I'm on my way." Tasha grabbed her emergency kit, the one she'd assembled when she started taking on hospital cases. As she hurried to her car, she felt the same sense of purpose that had originally drawn her to emergency medicine—the knowledge that her training could make the difference between life and death.

The drive to the Hendricks farm took her through country-side she was coming to know by heart. Rolling hills dotted with cattle, farmhouses with wide porches, the kind of landscape that had become synonymous with home. But today, the pastoral scene was marred by the urgent wail of sirens in the distance and the dark smoke rising from the direction of her destination.

She arrived to find controlled chaos. An ambulance was parked near the main barn, paramedics working around an overturned tractor that lay on its side like a sleeping giant. Grayson's truck was already there, and she could see him in the nearby paddock, moving among a small group of cattle with his characteristic calm efficiency.

"Dr. Jenkins!" One of the paramedics waved her over. "Thank God you're here. We've got Mr. Hendricks pinned under the tractor. He's conscious but in significant pain. Possible internal injuries, definitely some broken ribs."

Tasha immediately shifted into emergency mode, her training taking over as she approached the scene. Robert Hendricks, a man in his fifties whom she recognized from town, was indeed trapped beneath the heavy machinery. His face was pale with pain, but his eyes were alert and focused on her as she knelt beside him.

"Mr. Hendricks, I'm Dr. Jenkins. Can you tell me where it hurts?"

"Chest... ribs... hard to breathe," he managed between shallow breaths.

Tasha quickly assessed his vitals, noting the rapid pulse and decreased breath sounds on the left side. "Possible pneumotho-rax," she told the lead paramedic. "We need to get this tractor off him, but carefully. Any shift in position could worsen internal injuries."

As the firefighters worked to safely lift the tractor using hydraulic equipment, Tasha monitored Hendricks' condition, administering pain medication and preparing for the possibility that his lung might collapse completely once the pressure was removed.

"How are the cattle?" Hendricks asked through gritted teeth, his farmer's instincts overriding his pain.

"Dr. Mitchell is taking care of them," Tasha assured him. "Just focus on staying still and breathing as normally as you can."

Across the yard, she could see Grayson working with three injured cattle. Even from a distance, she could tell he was in his element—calm, methodical, completely focused on his patients. There was something beautiful about watching him work, the way he moved with such confidence and compassion.

"Tractor's clear!" the fire chief called out.

The moment the weight was lifted, Hendricks' breathing became even more labored. Tasha immediately placed her stethoscope on his chest, confirming her suspicions—his left lung had partially collapsed.

"I need to decompress his chest," she told the paramedics. "Get me a large bore needle and prep for transport."

Working quickly but carefully, Tasha inserted the needle between Hendricks' ribs, relieving the pressure that had been building in his chest cavity. Almost immediately, his breathing improved and some color returned to his face.

"Better?" she asked.

"Much," he gasped. "Thank you, Doc."

As the paramedics prepared to transport Hendricks to the hospital, Tasha walked over to check on Grayson's progress with the cattle. She found him bandaging a deep laceration on a young bull's flank while two other animals stood nearby, showing signs of minor injuries but nothing life-threatening.

"How's Mr. Hendricks?" Grayson asked without looking up from his work.

"Pneumothorax, some broken ribs, possible internal bleeding. They're transporting him now, but I think he'll be okay." She knelt beside him, automatically handing him supplies from his kit as he worked. "What happened here?"

"Tractor rolled when he was moving cattle. These three got caught in the fence when they spooked." He finished the bandage and stood, wiping sweat from his forehead with the back of his hand. "This boy here took the worst of it, but nothing that won't heal."

Tasha watched as he examined the bull's eyes, checking for signs of head trauma. There was something deeply satisfying about seeing him work—the same careful attention to detail, the same gentle competence she tried to bring to her own practice.

"Need any help?" she asked.

"Actually, yes. Can you hold his head while I check this leg? I think it might be fractured."

Working together, they examined the bull's injured limb. Tasha found herself automatically anticipating what Grayson needed, handing him supplies and helping to keep the animal calm while he worked. It felt natural, like they'd been doing this for years rather than for the first time.

"Hairline fracture," Grayson determined after careful palpation. "Nothing displaced, but he'll need to be confined for a few weeks while it heals."

"Will he be okay?"

"Should be fine. Bulls are tough, and this one's young and healthy."

As they finished treating the remaining cattle, Tasha became aware of how seamlessly they'd worked together. Their different medical training complemented each other perfectly—her knowledge of trauma and emergency medicine combined with his understanding of animal behavior and rural medicine created a partnership that was more effective than either of them working alone.

"That was impressive," said a voice behind them. They turned to find Sarah Hendricks, Robert's wife, approaching with tears in her eyes. "The way you two worked together, taking care of both Robert and the animals... I can't thank you enough."

"Just doing our jobs," Tasha said, but she felt a flush of pride at the recognition.

"No, it was more than that. Most doctors wouldn't have thought about the cattle, and most vets wouldn't have been able to help with Robert's injuries. Having both of you here..." Sarah wiped at her eyes. "It made all the difference."

Later, as they packed up their equipment, Grayson caught Tasha's eye. "That went well."

"It did. I'd forgotten how good it feels to work as part of a team like that."

"You were incredible back there. The way you handled the pneumothorax—I've never seen anything like that outside of a hospital."

Tasha felt warmth spread through her chest at his praise. "You weren't too shabby yourself. That bull could have done serious damage if you hadn't kept him calm."

They drove back into town in separate vehicles, but Tasha found herself thinking about their collaboration throughout the afternoon. When she got home that evening, she found Grayson on the back porch with two mugs of cocoa, clearly having had the same thoughts.

"So," he said as she settled beside him on the porch swing, "how did that feel?"

"Working together?" Tasha considered the question seriously. "Natural. Like we've been doing it for years."

"I was thinking the same thing. Your emergency training complemented my field experience perfectly."

"Dr. Martinez called while I was driving home," Tasha said, accepting the mug he offered. "He heard about today from the paramedics. Apparently, they were impressed with how we handled the dual emergency."

"Oh?"

"He wants to formalize our partnership. Set up protocols for situations where both human and animal medical care is needed." She took a sip of cocoa, studying Grayson's reaction. "What do you think?"

"I think it's a brilliant idea. We proved today that we work well together, and there are definitely situations where having both skill sets available could save lives."

"Both human and animal lives."

"Exactly."

They spent the next hour discussing the practical aspects of such a partnership. How they'd coordinate emergency responses, what equipment they'd need, how to establish protocols with the hospital and emergency services. But underneath the logistics, Tasha sensed something deeper—the recognition that their professional collaboration was as natural and effective as their personal relationship.

"You know what struck me most about today?" Tasha said as the sun began to set.

"What?"

"I wasn't scared. Six months ago, an emergency call like that would have sent me into a panic spiral. But today, I felt... competent. Present. Like I belonged there."

Grayson's hand found hers, squeezing gently. "You did belong there. You probably saved Robert Hendricks' life with that needle decompression."

"And you saved those cattle. Not to mention keeping everyone calm while we worked."

"We make a good team."

The simple statement carried weight beyond their professional collaboration. They did make a good team—in work, in life, in all the ways that mattered. Today had proven that their partnership extended beyond the personal into something that could benefit their entire community.

As they sat in comfortable silence, watching the first stars appear in the darkening sky, Tasha reflected on how much her life had changed. Six months ago, she'd been a broken doctor hiding from her past, convinced she'd never practice emergency medicine again. Now she was half of a medical partnership that could genuinely improve care for her adopted community.

"Grayson?"

"Mmm?"

"Thank you."

"For what?"

"For showing me that I could trust myself again. For being patient while I figured out who I wanted to be." She turned to face him directly. "For being the kind of partner who makes me better at everything I do."

He cupped her face gently, his thumb tracing her cheekbone. "Thank you for letting me be that partner. For both of us."

When he kissed her, soft and lingering in the gathering dusk, Tasha felt the deep contentment that came from finding exactly where she belonged. Not just in Sweetgum Meadows, not just in Grayson's life, but in work that challenged and fulfilled her, surrounded by people who valued what she had to offer.

Tomorrow they'd meet with Dr. Martinez to formalize their professional partnership. They'd establish protocols and coordinate with emergency services and probably field questions from curious colleagues. But tonight, she was simply grateful for the chance to build something meaningful with someone she loved, in a place that felt like home.

As they headed inside, Grayson's phone buzzed with a text from Earl: "Heard you and Dr. Jenkins saved the day at Hendricks' place. Good work, both of you."

"Word really does travel fast," Tasha observed.

"That's small-town life. But in this case, I don't mind."

"No," Tasha agreed, thinking about the satisfaction of work well done and recognition earned. "I don't mind either."

Because for the first time in her career, she was building something that felt sustainable—a practice that honored both her skills and her values, a partnership that strengthened rather than drained her, a life that felt authentically her own.

CHAPTER FOURTEEN

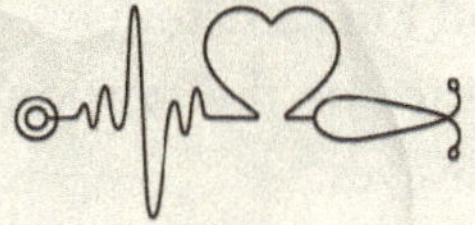

The morning after the Hendricks emergency, Grayson woke to the sound of soft humming from the kitchen. He lay still for a moment, absorbing the pleasure of knowing Tasha was there, that this wasn't a dream or a temporary arrangement but the reality of their shared life. The scent of coffee drifted upstairs, mixing with something that smelled like cinnamon and vanilla.

He found her at the stove, still in her pajamas with one of his flannel shirts thrown over them, flipping what appeared to be French toast. Her hair was pulled back in a messy bun, and she swayed slightly to music only she could hear.

"Morning," he said, wrapping his arms around her waist from behind.

"Perfect timing." She leaned back against his chest. "I was feeling domestic this morning. Thought we deserved a celebration breakfast after yesterday."

"What are we celebrating?"

"Our first official medical partnership case. The fact that we didn't completely mess it up. The way Sarah Hendricks looked at us like we'd performed a miracle." She turned in his arms, her eyes bright with residual excitement from their successful collaboration. "Pick your reason."

He kissed her forehead, then her nose, then her lips. "All of the above."

They ate breakfast on the back porch, discussing their upcoming meeting with Dr. Martinez. The morning was crisp but warming, with the kind of clear sky that promised a beautiful day. Grayson found himself studying Tasha's profile as she talked, noting the absence of the tension that had once lived permanently around her eyes.

"What?" she asked, catching him staring.

"Just thinking about how different you look now compared to when you first arrived."

"Different how?"

"Settled. Like you've stopped waiting for the other shoe to drop."

Tasha considered this, twirling her fork through the syrup on her plate. "I think you're right. I spent so long expecting disaster that I forgot what it felt like to just... exist without dread."

"And now?"

"Now I wake up looking forward to the day instead of just trying to survive it."

After breakfast, they drove separately to their respective jobs, but Grayson found his thoughts returning throughout the morning to their conversation. The woman he'd fallen in love with had been wounded, cautious, always ready to run. The woman who'd made French toast in his kitchen this morning was someone who'd found her place in the world and intended to keep it.

His first call was to the Morrison farm, where a pregnant mare was showing early signs of labor. As he examined the horse, his phone buzzed with a text from Tasha: "Meeting with Dr. Martinez went great. He's putting together a formal proposal for the hospital board. You're officially going to be on the emergency response roster."

The news filled him with pride—not just for the recognition of their partnership, but for what it represented. They were building something together, creating a professional collaboration that would outlast any individual case.

"Good news, Doc?" asked Jim Morrison, who'd been watching Grayson's expression as he read the message.

"Very good news. Dr. Jenkins and I are going to be working together more often on emergency cases."

"That's wonderful. You two make quite a team." Jim's weathered face creased into a knowing smile. "In more ways than one, from what I hear."

Grayson ducked his head but didn't deny it. The community's awareness of his relationship with Tasha had moved beyond speculation into acceptance, and he found he didn't mind the gentle teasing that came with it.

"She's... special," he said simply.

"That she is. And it's good to see you happy again."

The mare's labor progressed normally, resulting in a healthy foal by early afternoon. As Grayson cleaned up his equipment, his phone rang with a call from the veterinary supply company he'd been working with to expand his practice.

"Dr. Mitchell? This is Janet from Coleman Veterinary Supply. I have an update on that ultrasound equipment you inquired about."

Grayson stepped away from the barn to take the call. For months, he'd been considering investing in portable ultrasound equipment that would allow him to provide more advanced diagnostic services in the field. It was a significant financial commitment, but one that would greatly improve his ability to serve the community.

"The good news is we can offer you a payment plan that

would make it manageable," Janet continued. "The bad news is there's still a substantial upfront cost."

After discussing the details, Grayson hung up feeling both excited and apprehensive. The equipment would be a game-changer for his practice, but it represented a level of financial commitment that would tie him to Sweetgum Meadows for years to come. Six months ago, that prospect might have felt limiting. Now, it felt like putting down roots.

He was still pondering the decision when he arrived home that evening to find Tasha in the living room, surrounded by medical journals and legal pads covered with notes.

"Research?" he asked, settling beside her on the couch.

"Protocols. Dr. Martinez wants detailed procedures for different types of dual emergencies." She gestured to the papers scattered around her. "I'm trying to anticipate every possible scenario where we might need to coordinate care."

Grayson picked up one of her legal pads, scanning her neat handwriting. She'd outlined everything from farm equipment accidents to animal attacks to natural disasters, with detailed protocols for each situation.

"This is incredibly thorough."

"I want to get it right. This partnership could be a model for rural medical care. If we do this well, other communities might adopt similar programs."

The ambition in her voice made him love her even more. This wasn't just about their relationship or even their individual careers—it was about creating something that could help people and animals across rural America.

"Speaking of partnerships," he said, "I got a call about that ultrasound equipment today."

"The portable unit you've been wanting?"

"They can make it work financially, but it's still a big commitment." He turned to face her fully. "It would basically mean betting everything on this practice, on staying here long-term."

Tasha set down her pen and gave him her complete attention. "Is that what you want? To stay here long-term?"

"With you? Yes. Absolutely."

"Then what's holding you back?"

Grayson considered the question. "I guess I keep waiting for you to change your mind. To decide you miss the big city, or that small-town life isn't challenging enough, or that I'm not enough."

Tasha's expression softened. "Grayson, look around." She gestured to the room, to the journals and notes that represented her commitment to their shared work. "Look at what we're building together. Does this look like someone who's planning to leave?"

"No, it doesn't."

"I'm not going anywhere. This is my home now. You're my home."

The simple declaration hit him harder than any grand romantic gesture could have. This wasn't passion or infatuation —it was the quiet certainty of someone who'd found where she belonged.

"In that case," he said, pulling out his phone, "I'm going to order that equipment."

"Really?"

"Really. It's time I stopped hedging my bets and started investing in our future."

As he made the call to place the order, Tasha continued working on her protocols, but he caught her smiling as she wrote. When he finished the call, she looked up with obvious excitement.

"So we're both officially committed to staying in Sweetgum Meadows for the long haul?"

"Looks that way."

"Good. Because I have an idea I want to run by you."

She pulled out another legal pad, this one filled with sketches and calculations. "What if we formalized our partnership beyond just emergency calls? What if we created an integrated practice?"

Grayson leaned forward, studying her drawings. "What would that look like?"

"A clinic designed for both human and animal patients. Shared diagnostic equipment—like your new ultrasound. Coordinated care for agricultural families. Maybe even preventive programs that address both human and animal health simultaneously."

The scope of her vision was breathtaking. "That would be... revolutionary."

"It would also require significant investment and planning. But imagine the possibilities—comprehensive rural healthcare that actually understands the interconnection between people, animals, and land."

Grayson studied her sketches, his mind racing with the implications. It was ambitious beyond anything he'd ever considered, but it was also brilliant. Rural communities had unique healthcare needs that weren't adequately addressed by traditional models.

"You've really thought this through."

"I've been thinking about it since yesterday. Watching how we worked together, seeing how Sarah Hendricks reacted—it made me realize we could do so much more than just respond to emergencies."

"What would the timeline look like?"

"Years, probably. We'd need to build our reputations, secure funding, navigate regulatory requirements." She paused, watching his face carefully. "It's a big dream. Maybe too big."

"It's not too big." Grayson reached for her hand. "It's exactly the right size for two people who love what they do and want to make a real difference."

They spent the next two hours developing her idea, sketching possibilities and discussing practicalities. As the evening wore on, Grayson felt a growing excitement about their potential future. Not just as a couple, but as partners in something meaningful and innovative.

"You know what I love about this?" Tasha said as they finally cleared away the papers.

"What?"

"It's not just about us. It's about creating something that could outlast us, that could change how rural healthcare is delivered."

"Legacy."

"Exactly."

As they prepared for bed, Grayson reflected on the day's conversations. The ultrasound equipment order, Tasha's integrated practice vision, the quiet certainty with which they'd begun planning a future that stretched years into the distance—all of it pointed to the same truth.

They weren't just living together or even just building a relationship. They were creating a life, a practice, a contribution to their community that would define them for decades to come.

"Grayson?" Tasha said as they settled into bed.

"Mmm?"

"Thank you for believing in my crazy ideas."

"Thank you for having crazy ideas worth believing in."

She curled against his side, her head on his shoulder. "I never thought I'd feel this way again."

"What way?"

"Excited about the future. Like the best parts of my life are still ahead of me instead of behind me."

Grayson tightened his arms around her, feeling the same

excitement she described. For years after Leslie's death, he'd lived day to day, focused on just getting through rather than building toward anything. Now, with Tasha beside him and their shared dreams taking shape, the future felt full of possibility.

"I love you," he whispered into the darkness.

"I love you too."

As Tasha's breathing gradually evened out beside him, Grayson thought about the journey that had brought them here. Two wounded people who'd found healing in each other, two medical professionals who'd discovered they were better together than apart, two hearts that had learned to trust again.

Tomorrow they'd continue building their partnership, both personal and professional. They'd face new challenges and celebrate new successes. But tonight, he was simply grateful for the woman in his arms and the life they were creating together, one day at a time.

The future had never looked brighter.

CHAPTER FIFTEEN

Tasha was reviewing patient charts in Dr. Leighton's office when Margaret appeared in the doorway, her expression troubled.

"Dr. Jenkins? There's someone here to see you. He says he's your fiancé."

The words hit Tasha like ice water. Her pen slipped from suddenly nerveless fingers, clattering onto the desk. "My what?"

"He said fiancé. Brandon Morrison? He's quite insistent that he needs to speak with you immediately."

Tasha's stomach dropped to somewhere around her ankles. Brandon. Here. In Sweetgum Meadows. The two parts of her life—the broken past she'd fled and the whole future she was building—were about to collide in the worst possible way.

"Where is he?"

"In the waiting room. I told him you were with a patient, but he said he'd wait as long as necessary."

Tasha closed her eyes, trying to steady her breathing. Three months. Three months of peace, of building something real with Grayson, of feeling like herself again. And now Brandon had followed her here, bringing all the manipulation and toxicity she'd worked so hard to escape.

"Dr. Jenkins? Should I ask him to leave?"

"No." Tasha stood on unsteady legs. "I'll see him. But Margaret? If I'm not out in fifteen minutes, call Dr. Leighton. And... maybe call Dr. Mitchell too."

Margaret's eyebrows rose, but she nodded. "Of course."

The walk to the waiting room felt like a death march. Through the window, Tasha could see Brandon's familiar figure—tall, impeccably dressed in a suit that probably cost more than most people in Sweetgum Meadows made in a month. He was pacing, checking his expensive watch with the impatient energy that had once made her feel like she could never move fast enough to keep up with his expectations.

Now it just made her tired.

"Brandon." She kept her voice level as she entered the waiting room. "This is unexpected."

He turned, and for a moment his face lit up with genuine pleasure. "Tasha. God, you look... different. Good different. Healthy."

"What are you doing here?"

"I came to bring you home." He stepped closer, his cologne—expensive and cloying—filling the space between them. "I've missed you so much. We both have."

"We?"

"The hospital. The department. Me." His voice dropped to the intimate tone he'd once used to make her feel special. "Tasha, I made a mistake. Letting you leave was the biggest mistake of my life."

"I wasn't aware you'd had a choice in the matter."

Brandon's smile faltered slightly. "You're angry. I understand that. But I'm here to make things right."

Tasha studied his face, noting the calculated charm, the practiced sincerity. How had she ever thought this was love?

"Brandon, we broke up. You made it very clear that you couldn't handle being with someone who was 'wallowing' in trauma."

"I was frustrated. Scared. I didn't understand what you were going through." He reached for her hands, but she stepped back. "But I've learned. I've been in therapy, Tasha. Working on myself. I know I can be the partner you need now."

The lies came so smoothly, delivered with such apparent conviction, that for a moment Tasha felt the old self-doubt creep in. Maybe she had been too harsh. Maybe she hadn't given him enough credit for trying to understand.

Then she remembered Grayson's patient presence during her darkest moments, the way he'd held her while she cried about Dante Williams, the way he'd never once suggested she should just "get over it."

"I'm glad you're in therapy," she said carefully. "But Brandon, we're not getting back together."

"Because of him." Brandon's mask slipped for just a moment, revealing the possessive anger underneath. "I know about the veterinarian. It's a rebound, Tasha. A small-town fantasy that feels safe because it's not real."

Heat flared in Tasha's chest. "Don't."

"Don't what? Tell you the truth? You're hiding here, playing house with someone who could never understand what you're capable of. You're one of the most brilliant emergency physicians I've ever known, and you're wasting that gift in a place where the biggest emergency is probably a cow giving birth."

"You don't know anything about my life here."

"I know you're not practicing real medicine. I know you're settling for less than you deserve because you're scared." He stepped closer again, his voice taking on the persuasive tone that had once made her question her own perceptions. "But I also know the real Tasha Jenkins. The one who thrived on the challenge of a level-one trauma center. The one who saved lives that no one else could save."

"The one who lost Dante Williams."

"One patient, Tasha. One tragic case out of hundreds of successes. You can't let that define your entire career."

The familiar guilt tried to rise, but it felt weaker now, diluted by months of Patricia Williams' forgiveness and Grayson's unwavering belief in her abilities.

"It doesn't define my career," she said quietly. "But it taught me something important about the kind of doctor I want to be. The kind of life I want to live."

"Playing second fiddle to a country vet?"

The contempt in his voice made something snap inside her. "Grayson Mitchell is twice the man you'll ever be. He's brilliant, compassionate, and he's never once made me feel like I had to be perfect to earn his love."

Brandon's face hardened. "Love. You think this is love? Tasha, you've known him for what, three months? You were with me for two years."

"Two years of feeling like I was constantly failing to meet your expectations. Two years of walking on eggshells, afraid that any sign of weakness would make you lose interest."

"That's not how it was—"

"That's exactly how it was." Tasha's voice grew stronger with each word. "You couldn't handle seeing me struggle. The moment I became something other than your perfect, high-achieving trophy girlfriend, you checked out."

"I came here for you. I came to bring you home."

"This is my home."

"This?" Brandon gestured dismissively toward the window, beyond which the quiet streets of Sweetgum Meadows were visible. "This little town where nothing ever happens? Tasha, you're meant for greatness. You're meant to save lives in a major medical center, not patch up farmers and play happy homemaker."

"I am saving lives. And I'm building something meaningful

with someone who actually sees me as a whole person, not just a reflection of his own ambitions."

Brandon was quiet for a long moment, studying her face. When he spoke again, his voice had shifted to something more calculating. "I see. You really think you love him."

"I don't think anything. I know."

"Then you'll want to protect him."

The subtle threat in his tone made Tasha's blood run cold. "What's that supposed to mean?"

"Small-town veterinarians probably don't have the resources to handle... complications. Legal complications, for instance."

"Brandon, what are you talking about?"

"The Williams case isn't as closed as you think it is. There are still questions being asked, still lawyers sniffing around. It would be a shame if those questions led to an investigation that somehow implicated your new boyfriend."

Tasha stared at him, horrified by the naked manipulation. "You're threatening Grayson."

"I'm stating facts. Medical malpractice cases have a way of expanding, especially when insurance companies start looking for other parties to blame. Emergency veterinary procedures, consultations that blur the line between human and animal medicine... it could get very messy for someone without proper legal protection."

"You're lying. There is no Williams case. Patricia Williams told me herself that no legal action was ever filed."

Brandon's smile turned cold. "Patricia Williams doesn't speak for the entire family. Or for the hospital's insurance company. Or for the state medical board if someone were to file a new complaint."

The implications hit her like a physical blow. He was threatening to manufacture legal trouble that could destroy not just her career but Grayson's as well. All because she'd refused to come back to him.

"You're despicable."

"I'm practical. And I'm offering you a way to avoid all of this unpleasantness." His voice softened again, the practiced charm sliding back into place. "Come home with me, Tasha. Resume your real career. Leave this small-town fantasy behind before it gets complicated for everyone involved."

Tasha felt the old familiar panic rising—the sense that she was trapped, that any choice she made would lead to disaster. For a moment, she was back in Atlanta, doubting herself, accepting Brandon's version of reality because it was easier than fighting.

Then she thought of Grayson's steady presence, of the life they were building together, of the way he'd believed in her even when she couldn't believe in herself.

"No."

"Tasha—"

"No. I'm not going anywhere with you. And if you think you can threaten the people I love to manipulate me, you're about to learn just how wrong you are."

Brandon's mask slipped completely, revealing the ugly entitlement underneath. "You're making a mistake. A big one."

"The only mistake I made was staying with you as long as I did."

"This isn't over."

"Yes, it is." Tasha moved toward the door, then turned back. "And Brandon? If you do anything to hurt Grayson or anyone else in this town, I will make it my life's mission to expose exactly what kind of person you really are. I have documentation of your harassment, witnesses to your threats, and I'm not the scared, guilty woman you remember. Try me."

She walked out of the waiting room without looking back, her heart pounding but her resolve absolute. In the hallway, she nearly collided with Dr. Leighton, who took one look at her face and frowned.

"Everything alright?"

"It will be. Is Margaret still at the front desk?"

"Yes, why?"

"I need her to call the police. I want to file a report about threats and harassment."

Dr. Leighton's expression grew serious. "What kind of threats?"

"The kind that makes it clear this isn't just a personal visit."

As they walked toward the front desk, Tasha felt something settle inside her—not fear, but fierce protectiveness. Brandon had made a crucial miscalculation in threatening Grayson. He'd assumed she was still the woman who could be manipulated through guilt and fear.

But that woman was gone. In her place was someone who'd learned to fight for what mattered, someone who'd found a home worth defending.

And she was done running.

Through the window, she could see Brandon getting into a rental car, his face dark with fury. He'd expected her to crumble, to follow him back to Atlanta like a chastened child.

Instead, he was leaving empty-handed while she stayed exactly where she belonged.

Tasha pulled out her phone and typed a quick text to Grayson: "Need to talk when you get home. Everything's okay, but something happened today that you should know about."

Then she called Margaret over and began the process of documenting Brandon's threats. Because if he thought he could intimidate her into abandoning the life she'd built, he was about to discover just how much fight she had left in her.

The old Tasha might have run. The new Tasha was standing her ground.

CHAPTER SIXTEEN

Grayson was suturing a laceration on a young colt's leg when his phone buzzed with Tasha's text. The careful neutrality of her message—"everything's okay, but something happened"—immediately put him on edge. In his experience, when someone led with "everything's okay," it usually meant the opposite.

He finished the procedure with methodical care, his mind racing through possibilities. An emergency at the clinic? Problems with their partnership proposal? Something from her past in Atlanta?

The drive home felt interminable. When he finally pulled into their driveway, he found Tasha pacing on the front porch, her phone pressed to her ear. She was speaking in the crisp, professional tone she used for serious medical situations.

"Yes, I understand the process. Tomorrow morning is fine for filing the formal complaint." She paused, listening. "No, I don't think he'll try to contact me again tonight, but I'll call if anything changes."

She ended the call as Grayson approached, her expression grim but determined.

"Who was that?" he asked, studying her face for clues.

"The police station. I filed a report this afternoon." She took a deep breath. "Brandon showed up at the clinic today."

The name hit Grayson like a physical blow. Brandon. The ex-fiancé who'd been manipulating Tasha from Atlanta, the man whose lies had driven her to question everything about her medical abilities.

"What did he want?"

"Me to come back to Atlanta with him. When I refused, he threatened you."

Anger flared in Grayson's chest, hot and immediate. "He threatened me?"

"He implied that he could manufacture legal trouble for you related to our professional partnership. Suggested that medical malpractice cases could be expanded to include veterinarians who consult on human emergencies."

The calculated nature of the threat made Grayson's hands clench into fists. This wasn't just about winning Tasha back—it was about using fear and intimidation to control her, regardless of who else got hurt in the process.

"What did you tell him?"

"I told him no. Absolutely, unequivocally no." Tasha's voice grew stronger with each word. "And I told him that if he tried to hurt you or anyone else in this town, I'd make it my mission to expose exactly what kind of person he really is."

Pride swelled in Grayson's chest alongside the anger. "Good for you."

"I documented everything with the police." She paused, watching his face carefully. "Grayson, I'm so sorry he dragged you into this."

"You have nothing to apologize for." He pulled her into his arms, feeling the slight tremor in her shoulders. "Are you okay?"

"I'm furious. And scared. Not for me, but for you, for what

he might try to do." Her voice dropped to a whisper. "I couldn't bear it if my past hurt you."

"Hey." Grayson cupped her face, forcing her to meet his eyes. "We're going to handle this together. Whatever he tries, we'll face it together."

"But what if he actually does something? What if he finds a way to cause legal problems for your practice?"

"Then we'll deal with that too. Tasha, I'm not going anywhere. Some entitled ex-boyfriend from Atlanta isn't going to scare me away from the best thing that's ever happened to me."

They went inside, settling on the couch where Tasha recounted the entire encounter in detail. With each revelation—Brandon's attempts at manipulation, his dismissive comments about their relationship, his threats against Grayson's practice—the anger in Grayson's chest burned hotter.

"I should have been there," he said when she finished.

"No. I needed to handle this myself. To prove to myself that I could stand up to him without falling apart."

"And you did. You were incredible."

"I was terrified the whole time. But I kept thinking about us, about the life we're building, about how patient you've been while I figured out how to trust again." Her hands found his, squeezing tightly. "I wasn't going to let him destroy that."

They spent the evening discussing practical matters—the police report, potential legal protections, ways to document their professional protocols to prevent any future challenges. But underneath the logistics, Grayson sensed Tasha processing something deeper.

"You know what the strangest part was?" she said as they prepared for bed.

"What?"

"How small he seemed. I spent so many months thinking of Brandon as this powerful force who could destroy my life with a phone call. But seeing him today, listening to his threats... he's just a man. A petty, manipulative man who can't stand that I chose someone else."

"You're stronger than you were when you left Atlanta."

"We're stronger. This whole thing made me realize something." She turned to face him fully. "I'm not the same person who was with Brandon. That woman was so desperate for approval that she let him chip away at her confidence piece by piece. But the woman I am now? The woman you helped me become? She doesn't negotiate with bullies."

The next morning, Grayson woke to find Tasha already dressed and making coffee with determined efficiency.

"Early day?" he asked.

"I want to get to the police station when they open. The sooner we get this officially documented, the better."

They drove into town together, planning to head straight to the police station. But as they approached, Tasha suddenly went rigid in the passenger seat.

"Oh no."

"What?" Grayson followed her gaze to see a man in an expensive suit standing near the police station entrance.

"That's Brandon."

Grayson's stomach clenched as he took in the tall, impeccably dressed figure. So this was the man who'd manipulated and threatened Tasha, who'd tried to destroy her confidence when she needed support most.

Brandon spotted their truck and began walking toward them with the confident stride of someone who believed he held all the cards.

"Tasha. I was hoping we could talk again. I think there were some misunderstandings yesterday."

"There were no misunderstandings." Tasha's voice was ice cold. "And I have nothing more to say to you."

Brandon's gaze shifted to Grayson, taking in his height, his broad shoulders, the protective way he positioned himself slightly in front of Tasha.

"You must be the veterinarian." Brandon's tone carried carefully calculated disdain. "I have to say, I'm not impressed. Is this really what Tasha's settling for? A country vet who plays doctor with farm animals?"

"Brandon, stop." Tasha's warning carried real heat.

But Grayson stepped forward, his own anger finally finding its voice. "Let me make something very clear. Tasha isn't settling for anything. She chose to build a life here, with me, because she's smart enough to recognize the difference between real love and manipulation."

"Real love?" Brandon laughed, the sound harsh and mocking. "You've known her for what, three months? I was with her for two years. I know her in ways you never will."

"You knew a version of her that you tried to control and diminish. I know the woman she actually is."

"The woman she actually is," Brandon repeated, his mask beginning to slip. "Let me tell you what she actually is. She's a brilliant surgeon who's wasting her talents in this backwater town because she's too scared to face her responsibilities."

"She's a doctor who cares more about healing people than impressing colleagues. She's someone brave enough to start over when her life stopped working. She's the strongest person I've ever met."

Brandon's face flushed with anger. "You don't know what you're talking about. You don't know about her history, about the mistakes she's made."

"I know about Dante Williams. I know about the investigation, about the trauma she endured, about the guilt she carried." Grayson's voice dropped to a dangerous quiet. "And I know that instead of supporting her through the worst period of her life, you made it worse by questioning her judgment and her character."

"I tried to help her move on—"

"You tried to make her pretend it never happened because dealing with her pain was inconvenient for you."

"That's not—"

"It's exactly what happened." Tasha's voice cut through their confrontation like a blade. "Grayson's right. When I needed support, you gave me ultimatums. When I needed understanding, you gave me judgment."

Brandon turned back to her, desperation creeping into his voice. "I made mistakes. I admit that. But I learned from them. I can be better."

"Maybe you can. But not with me. We're done, Brandon. We've been done for months."

"Because of him." Brandon's gaze swung back to Grayson, pure venom now. "This is all about him, isn't it? You think you've found some kind of fairy tale romance with the local animal doctor."

"I found someone who makes me better instead of smaller," Tasha said quietly.

"You're deluding yourself. What happens when the novelty wears off? When you realize you've buried yourself in a town where nothing ever happens?"

"Then I'll be grateful every day that I chose a peaceful life with someone I love over the chaos of trying to meet impossible standards."

Brandon stared at her for a long moment, something shifting in his expression. "You really mean that."

"I really do."

"Then you're not the woman I thought you were."

"No," Tasha agreed. "I'm not. I'm better."

For a moment, Grayson thought Brandon might actually walk away. But then his face hardened again, the entitled anger returning.

"This isn't over. I meant what I said about legal complications. One phone call to the right lawyer, one complaint to the state medical board about unlicensed practice—"

"Enough." Grayson's voice carried a quiet authority that made Brandon step back. "You've threatened her, you've threatened me, and you've made it clear that you're willing to abuse the legal system to get your way. But here's what you haven't considered."

He pulled out his phone, tapping the screen. "I've been recording this entire conversation. Everything you just said about manufacturing legal trouble, about filing false complaints —it's all documented."

Brandon's face fell slack. "You can't—"

"I can and I did. And if you ever contact Tasha again, if you ever come back to this town, if you ever follow through on any of these threats, this recording goes to the police, to the Georgia State Bar, and to the administration at Emory University Hospital."

"You're bluffing."

"Try me."

The two men stared at each other for a long moment, and Grayson saw the exact moment when Brandon realized he'd lost. The blustering confidence crumbled, leaving behind a man who'd built his identity on control and found himself suddenly powerless.

"This is ridiculous," Brandon muttered, but the fight had gone out of him. "Fine. Keep your little small-town fantasy. When it falls apart, don't come crying to me."

He stalked back to his rental car, his movements sharp with frustrated anger. As he drove away, Tasha sagged against Grayson's side.

"Is it really over?" she asked.

"It's over." He wrapped his arms around her, feeling the tension slowly leave her body. "He's not coming back."

"How can you be sure?"

"Because bullies like Brandon are cowards at heart. They only attack when they think they can win. Now he knows he can't."

As they walked into the police station to complete their report, Grayson felt a deep satisfaction. Not because he'd won some kind of territorial dispute, but because Tasha had finally, definitively closed the door on a chapter of her life that had caused her so much pain.

"Grayson?" she said as they reached the station's entrance.

"Yeah?"

"Thank you. For defending me, for protecting us, for being exactly the kind of man worth fighting for."

He kissed her forehead, breathing in the familiar scent of her hair. "Thank you for being worth the fight."

As they completed the report, Grayson knew they'd turned a corner. Whatever challenges lay ahead, they'd face them as partners—equal, committed, and unshakeable in their love for each other.

The past was finally, truly behind them. And the future stretched ahead, bright with possibility.

CHAPTER SEVENTEEN

The silence in the truck as they drove home from the police station was profound. Tasha sat in the passenger seat, her hands still slightly shaky from the morning's confrontation. Part of her couldn't quite believe it was over—that she'd actually stood up to Brandon, that Grayson had defended her so fiercely, that Brandon had finally backed down and left town.

"You okay?" Grayson's voice was gentle, concerned.

"I think so." She turned to look at him, taking in his still-tense posture, the protective way his eyes kept checking the mirrors as if Brandon might reappear. "Are you okay?"

"I'm furious," he said honestly. "Not at you," he added quickly, seeing her expression. "At him. At the way he talked to you, the way he dismissed our relationship, the casual cruelty of those threats."

Tasha reached over and took his hand, feeling the slight tremor of residual adrenaline. "I've never had anyone defend me like that before."

"What do you mean?"

"With Brandon, I was always fighting alone. Even when we

were together, if someone criticized me or questioned my judgment, he'd either agree with them or stay silent. But you..." She squeezed his fingers. "You didn't just defend me. You defended us."

"Of course I did. We're a team."

The simple certainty in his voice made her chest tight with emotion. "I love you," she said quietly. "I love that you recorded that conversation, that you were thinking three steps ahead while I was just trying not to fall apart."

"You weren't falling apart. You were incredible back there."

"I was terrified."

"But you didn't let that stop you. You told him exactly where he could go with his manipulation and threats."

Sheriff Jonathan Michaels had taken their statement seriously, documenting Brandon's threats thoroughly and assuring them that the harassment complaint would be filed properly. "Men like this often think small-town police won't take them seriously," she'd said. "They're usually wrong about that."

By the time they pulled into their driveway, Tasha's phone was buzzing with concerned texts. Brandi, Mrs. Bridges, Earl—somehow word had already spread through Sweetgum Meadows' efficient communication network.

"That's Sweetgum for you," Grayson observed, reading over her shoulder as another message came in.

"I should probably respond to these before people start showing up at our house with casseroles and concerned looks."

"Would that be such a bad thing?"

The question made her pause. Six months ago, the idea of a community rallying around her would have felt overwhelming, suffocating. Now it felt like protection, like belonging to something larger than herself.

"No," she said, surprised by how much she meant it. "It wouldn't be bad at all."

They settled on the back porch with coffee, the familiar view of rolling pasture land helping to center her after the morning's chaos. Grayson seemed to sense her need to process, sitting quietly beside her as she worked through her thoughts.

"I keep thinking about something he said," she finally ventured.

"What?"

"That I was wasting my talents here. That I was settling for less than I deserved." She turned to face him. "For a minute, when he first said it, I almost believed him."

Grayson's expression grew serious. "And now?"

"Now I realize he has it backwards. In Atlanta, I was wasting my talents trying to be someone I wasn't. Here, I'm using them in ways that actually matter."

"How so?"

Tasha considered her answer carefully. "In Atlanta, success was measured by how many high-profile cases you handled, how many procedures you could perform in a shift, how impressive your statistics looked on paper. But here... here it's about whether Mrs. Patterson feels comfortable coming in for her follow-up appointments. Whether I can help a farmer understand his injury well enough to prevent it from happening again. Whether a scared kid feels safe while I'm stitching up their cuts."

"That sounds like pretty meaningful work to me."

"It is. And the partnership we're building—that integrated approach to rural healthcare—that could genuinely change how medical care is delivered in communities like this one." She leaned back against the porch swing. "Brandon sees that as settling because it's not about prestige or recognition. But it's about impact. Real impact."

Her phone buzzed again, this time with a call from Brandi. Tasha answered, putting it on speaker.

"Are you okay?" Brandi's voice was sharp with concern. "Margaret told Courtney that some man in a suit was at the clinic yesterday making threats, and then India saw you when she was passing the police station this morning—"

"I'm fine," Tasha interrupted gently. "We're both fine. It was my ex-fiancé from Atlanta. He showed up trying to convince me to go back with him."

"And?"

"And I told him exactly where he could go with that idea."

"Good. Do I need to organize a posse? Because I will absolutely organize a posse."

Despite everything, Tasha found herself laughing. "No posse necessary. He's gone, and he won't be back."

"You sure about that?"

Tasha glanced at Grayson, who nodded encouragingly. "I'm sure. But thank you for being ready to ride to my rescue."

"That's what friends do. We're having an emergency book club meeting tonight at my house. Seven o'clock. Non-negotiable."

After Brandi hung up, Grayson smiled. "Emergency book club meeting?"

"Apparently. Which means I'll be subjected to detailed interrogation, unsolicited advice, and probably enough food to feed a small army."

"Sounds terrible."

"It sounds perfect, actually." She curled up against his side. "Six months ago, the idea of that many people caring about my problems would have sent me into a panic. Now it just feels like home."

They spent the afternoon in comfortable routine—Grayson had calls to make about his expanding practice, and Tasha caught up on patient charts. But underneath the normalcy, she felt something shifting inside her. The confrontation with Brandon had crystallized something important.

She wasn't the same woman who'd fled Atlanta in fear and shame. That woman had been beaten down by guilt and manipulation, convinced she was broken beyond repair. The woman she was now—the woman Grayson's love had helped her become—was stronger, clearer about what she wanted and what she wouldn't tolerate.

Around five o'clock, as she was getting ready to leave for Brandi's, her phone rang. Dr. Martinez from the hospital.

"Dr. Jenkins? I hope I'm not calling at a bad time."

"Not at all. What can I do for you?"

"I had an interesting conversation today with someone claiming to be investigating your medical credentials. A Brandon Morrison from Atlanta?"

Tasha's blood ran cold. "What did he want?"

"He was asking questions about your work here, specifically about your partnership with Dr. Mitchell. Wanted to know if you were practicing outside your scope, if there were any concerns about the dual emergency protocols we've been developing."

"What did you tell him?"

"I told him that your credentials were impeccable, your work was exemplary, and that if he had official concerns, he could file them through proper channels with appropriate documentation." Dr. Martinez's voice carried a note of dry amusement. "He seemed frustrated by that response."

"I'm so sorry he contacted you. He's my ex-fiancé, and he's been trying to manipulate me into returning to Atlanta."

"I figured it was something like that. Don't worry about it— we get inquiries like this sometimes from disgruntled former colleagues or personal contacts. They never amount to anything when the doctor in question is doing good work."

After she hung up, Tasha felt a mixture of anger and vindication. Brandon had actually followed through on his threats, trying to manufacture problems for her professional life. But instead of the catastrophe he'd predicted, his inquiry had only highlighted her strong standing with the hospital.

She found Grayson in the barn, checking on a horse he'd treated earlier in the week.

"Brandon called Dr. Martinez today," she said without preamble.

Grayson's hands stilled on the horse's flank. "What did he want?"

"To fish for information about our partnership, hoping to find something he could use against us." She leaned against the stall door. "Dr. Martinez shut him down completely and said inquiries like that never amount to anything when the doctor is doing good work."

"So his threats were empty."

"Completely empty. He was bluffing, hoping to scare me into compliance."

Grayson finished his examination and turned to face her fully. "How do you feel about that?"

"Angry that he tried. Relieved that it didn't work. Proud that I've built something here that can't be destroyed by his petty revenge attempts."

"You should be proud. You've created a practice and a reputation that speak for themselves."

At Brandi's house that evening, Tasha found herself surrounded by the warm chaos of the emergency book club meeting. Mrs. Bridges had brought her famous cookies, India had contributed ice cream, Joanne brought drinks, and Courtney arrived with a casserole "just in case."

"Alright," Brandi said once everyone was settled in her living room, "tell us everything. And don't leave out any details."

Tasha recounted the previous day's clinic visit and that morning's confrontation, watching her friends' expressions grow increasingly indignant on her behalf.

"What an absolute toad," India declared when she finished. "Who does he think he is, showing up here like he owns you?"

"The kind of man who can't accept that a woman might

choose someone else," Mrs. Bridges said grimly. "I've met his type before."

"But you stood up to him," Courtney added admiringly. "You didn't let him intimidate you into going back."

"I almost did," Tasha admitted. "For a moment, when he was talking about legal threats, I felt that old panic starting. The urge to do whatever it took to make the problem go away."

"What stopped you?" Joanne asked.

"Grayson. This community. The life we've built together." She looked around at the concerned faces surrounding her. "I realized I had something worth fighting for instead of just something to lose."

"Good," Mrs. Bridges said firmly. "That's exactly right."

"And now he's gone for good?" India asked.

"He's gone. Grayson made it very clear that any further contact would result in serious legal consequences."

"I like that man more every day," Brandi declared. "The way he defended you this morning—that's what real love looks like."

They spent the next hour dissecting every aspect of the confrontation, offering advice, support, and increasingly creative suggestions for what they'd like to do to Brandon if he ever showed his face in Sweetgum Meadows again. By the time Tasha left, she felt lighter than she had all day.

At home, she found Grayson reading on the couch, but he looked up immediately when she entered.

"How was the emergency meeting?"

"Perfect. Exactly what I needed." She settled beside him, curling into his warmth. "They were properly outraged on my behalf and full of threats about what they'd do if Brandon ever comes back."

"I like your friends."

"They like you too. Brandi said the way you defended me this morning is what real love looks like."

"She's right."

Tasha tilted her head to look at him. "Is she?"

"Real love means protecting what matters. Fighting for the people who matter. You matter, Tasha. More than anything."

The simple declaration made her eyes fill with tears. "I've never felt protected before. Not the way I do with you."

"You'll never have to face something like this alone again."

As they prepared for bed, Tasha reflected on everything that had happened over the past two days. Brandon's arrival had felt like a crisis, a threat to everything she'd built. But in the end, it had only proven how strong her new life actually was.

She had a career that fulfilled her, a community that supported her, and a man who loved her enough to fight for their future together. Brandon's manipulation tactics had no power over someone who knew her own worth.

"Grayson?" she said as they settled into bed.

"Mmm?"

"Thank you. For standing with me, for believing in me, for showing me what it feels like to be truly loved."

"Thank you for being brave enough to choose this life. To choose us."

As Tasha drifted off to sleep in his arms, she felt something she'd never experienced before: complete security. Not because her life was perfect or without challenges, but because she'd found someone who would face those challenges beside her.

Brandon's visit had been meant to destabilize her, to make her question her choices. Instead, it had only confirmed that she was exactly where she belonged.

With Grayson. In Sweetgum Meadows. Building a future that was entirely, authentically her own.

CHAPTER EIGHTEEN

Three days had passed since Brandon's departure, and life in Sweetgum Meadows had settled back into its comfortable rhythm. Grayson was reviewing supply orders for his practice when his phone rang with a number he recognized immediately—his sister Caroline calling from Nashville.

"Hey, Caroline. What's going on?"

"Gray! Perfect timing. I have a favor to ask, and before you say no, hear me out completely."

Grayson smiled at his sister's familiar rapid-fire delivery. Caroline had always been the family organizer, the one who coordinated holidays and kept everyone connected despite busy schedules and geographic distance.

"I'm listening."

"Okay, so you know how I've been dying to meet this mysterious Tasha you've been telling us about, right? Well, it turns out we're driving through Georgia next week on our way to David's conference in Savannah. The kids are out of school for a long weekend, and we thought we could make a little family road trip out of it."

"That sounds nice, but what's the favor?"

"Could we possibly stop by Sweetgum Meadows to visit Friday night? Maybe meet this woman who's got our stoic brother so smitten? David could use the break from driving, and the kids are curious about Uncle Grayson's girlfriend."

The word 'girlfriend' felt inadequate for what Tasha meant to him, but Grayson found himself smiling at his sister's enthusiasm. "When were you thinking?"

"Friday evening? We could arrive around dinner time, spend the evening getting to know Tasha, and then head out Saturday morning. I found this charming bed and breakfast online—the Sweetgum Bed & Breakfast? It looks perfect for a family stay."

Grayson smiled, knowing Caroline would love Rochelle and Benjamin's place. "That's Benjamin and Rochelle's B and B. She used to own the diner in town before she got married to the owner of the bed and breakfast. You'll love them."

"Perfect! So what do you think? Would Friday work?"

Grayson's first instinct was to say yes—he'd been wanting his family to meet Tasha. But then he considered the timing. She was just starting to feel settled after the Brandon incident, and meeting his family might feel overwhelming.

"Can I talk to Tasha and call you back?"

"Of course. But Gray? I really hope she says yes. I'm dying to meet the woman who made you happy again."

After ending the call, Grayson sat for a moment, thinking about how to approach the subject with Tasha. They'd talked about his family in general terms, but the prospect of an actual meeting might feel daunting.

He found her in the kitchen, reviewing patient charts while eating lunch. She looked up as he entered, noting his expression immediately.

"Everything okay? You look like you're processing something."

"That was Caroline. My sister from Nashville."

"The one with the kids?"

"That's the one. She and her family are driving to Savannah next week for her husband's conference, and they want to stop by here Friday evening. To meet you."

Tasha's fork paused halfway to her mouth. "Meet me?"

"Just for dinner. They'd arrive around dinner time and stay at the Sweetgum Bed & Breakfast overnight, then leave Saturday morning." He settled into the chair across from her. "But if you're not ready for that, or if it feels like too much after everything with Brandon—"

"What are they like? Your family."

The question surprised him. He'd expected immediate anxiety or deflection, not genuine curiosity.

"Caroline's the organizer. She's a nurse practitioner, married to David, who's a college professor. They have two kids— Emma's twelve and Jake's nine. Caroline's got a protective streak and a great sense of humor."

"What have you told them about me?"

"That you're a doctor from Atlanta who moved here for a fresh start. That you're brilliant and kind and you make me happier than I've been in years." He paused. "That I'm in love with you."

Her expression softened. "You told them you love me?"

"I told them I love you."

She was quiet for a long moment, and Grayson could practically see her working through the implications. Meeting his family would be a significant step, a declaration that their relationship was serious and permanent.

"What if they don't like me?"

"They'll love you. How could they not?"

"What if I say something wrong? What if they think I'm not good enough for you?"

Grayson reached across the table and took her hand. "Tasha, look at me."

She met his eyes reluctantly.

"You are more than good enough. You're extraordinary. And my family is going to see that within five minutes of meeting you."

"I've never been particularly good with families. Brandon's parents barely tolerated me, and my own family..." She trailed off, old pain flickering across her features.

"This isn't Brandon's family. And it's definitely not your family. Caroline and David are good people who care about the people I care about."

"And you think they'll like me?"

"I know they will. But more importantly, do you want to meet them?"

Tasha considered the question seriously. "Yes," she said finally. "Yes, I do. I want to be part of your life completely, and that includes your family."

"Are you sure? We can wait if you need more time."

"I'm sure. Nervous, but sure." She squeezed his hand. "Besides, if we're going to build a life together, I should probably meet the people who helped make you who you are."

Relief flooded through Grayson, along with excitement at the prospect of his two worlds finally intersecting. "I'll call Caroline back and tell her yes."

"Wait." Tasha's grip on his hand tightened. "What should I cook? What do they like to eat? Should I clean the house? What if—"

"Breathe," Grayson interrupted gently. "We'll figure it all out together."

The rest of the afternoon was spent in pleasant preparation. Tasha insisted on deep-cleaning the entire house, despite Grayson's assurances that Caroline wouldn't judge them for a little dust.

"It's not about judgment," Tasha explained as she reorganized the linen closet. "It's about making a good first impression."

"You could serve them cereal for dinner and they'd still love you if you make me happy."

"That's sweet, but I'm still deep-cleaning this bathroom."

They spent Thursday evening planning the menu. Tasha wanted to cook something impressive but not so complicated that she'd be stressed. Grayson said they would cook together. They settled on his grandmother's pot roast recipe, which would be hearty enough for a family with children but elegant enough to showcase their cooking skills.

"What should I wear?" she asked as they prepared for bed Thursday night.

"Whatever makes you comfortable."

"That's not helpful. Should I look professional? Casual? What message am I trying to send?"

Grayson pulled her into his arms, amused by her nervousness. "The message you're trying to send is that you're the woman I love. Everything else is just details."

"You're not nervous at all, are you?"

"About my family meeting you? Not even a little."

"Why not?"

"Because I know how this story ends. They're going to love you, you're going to love them, and afterward you'll wonder why you were so worried."

Friday morning brought a flurry of last-minute preparations. Tasha started the pot roast early with Grayson's help, filled the house with flowers from their garden, and changed her outfit three times before settling on a simple dress that was both comfortable and flattering.

"You look beautiful," Grayson assured her as she checked her reflection in the hallway mirror for the fourth time.

"I look nervous."

"You look perfect."

Around noon, Caroline called to confirm their arrival time and ask about dinner preferences. "The kids aren't picky eaters, but Jake's going through a phase where he only likes foods that aren't green."

"No green foods. Got it," Tasha said when Grayson relayed the message. "What about Caroline and David?"

"Caroline will eat anything except brussels sprouts. David's vegetarian."

Tasha's eyes widened. "Vegetarian? The pot roast is beef!"

"It's fine. We'll make sure there are plenty of vegetarian sides. David's used to adapting."

"Maybe I should make something else entirely—"

"Tasha." Grayson caught her hands as she started to pace. "It's going to be fine. They're coming to meet you, not to judge your cooking."

"Easy for you to say. They already love you unconditionally."

"And they're going to love you too. Maybe not unconditionally at first, but that'll change quickly."

Despite her anxiety, the afternoon passed pleasantly. They set the table with their best dishes, arranged flowers in the living room, and made sure everything was welcoming. Grayson called Rochelle to let her know his family would be checking in later that evening.

"Oh how wonderful!" Rochelle's warm voice carried genuine excitement. "We'd love to meet your sister and her family. Benjamin just finished renovating the family suite—it'll be perfect for them."

"Thanks, Rochelle. They're good people. You'll like them."

"I'm sure we will. And Grayson? It's so nice to see you building these connections again. Tasha's been wonderful for you."

As evening approached, Tasha's nervous energy reached new heights.

"What if they ask about my family? About why I left Atlanta? About Brandon?"

"Then you tell them as much or as little as you're comfortable sharing. Caroline's a nurse—she understands that people have complicated histories."

"What if the kids don't like me?"

"Emma and Jake are going to adore you. Emma's at the age where she's fascinated by strong women, and Jake loves anyone who pays attention to his baseball card collection."

"You think I'm strong?"

The question surprised him. "Of course I do. You're one of the strongest people I know."

"I don't feel strong right now. I feel terrified."

Grayson pulled her close, breathing in the familiar scent of her hair.

"There is absolutely nothing to worry about."

"What if they think I'm not good enough for you?"

"Then they're not as smart as I think they are. Which is impossible, because my sister is universally brilliant."

At five-thirty, headlights appeared in their driveway. Tasha immediately went still, her hand finding Grayson's.

"They're here," she whispered.

"They're here," he agreed. "Ready?"

She took a deep breath, squaring her shoulders in the way that meant she was gathering her courage. "Ready."

As they walked to the front door together, Grayson felt a deep sense of rightness about this moment. His family was about to meet the woman he wanted to spend his life with, and despite Tasha's nervousness, he knew this was just the beginning of her integration into the larger circle of people who loved him.

Through the window, he could see Caroline getting out of their SUV, followed by David and the kids. Caroline spotted him and waved enthusiastically, her smile bright even from a distance.

"Here we go," he murmured to Tasha, squeezing her hand once more before opening the door to welcome his family into their home.

The future had never felt brighter or more certain.

CHAPTER NINETEEN

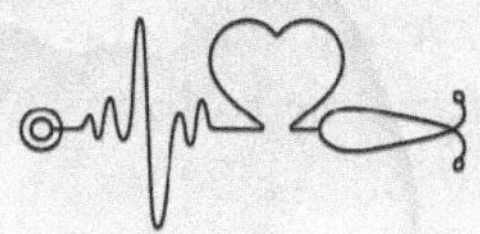

The moment Grayson opened the front door, Tasha was enveloped in a whirlwind of energy that could only be described as pure Mitchell family enthusiasm. Caroline stepped forward first—a petite woman with Grayson's warm brown eyes, her face lit up with genuine excitement.

"Grayson!" She threw her arms around her brother, then immediately turned to Tasha with the kind of smile that made instant friendship feel inevitable. "And you must be Tasha. I'm Caroline, and I am so happy to finally meet you."

Before Tasha could respond, she found herself pulled into a warm hug that somehow managed to be both enthusiastic and completely natural. Over Caroline's shoulder, she caught Grayson's amused expression and felt some of her nervousness begin to ease.

"It's wonderful to meet you too," Tasha managed as Caroline stepped back.

"This is my husband David," Caroline continued, gesturing to the tall, bearded man stretching beside their SUV. "And those are our children—Emma and Jake."

David approached with a friendly smile, extending his hand.

"Great to meet you, Tasha. Caroline's been chattering about meeting you nonstop."

"Dad, I told you not to tell her that," came a voice from behind him. Emma, a twelve-year-old with her mother's features but her father's height, rolled her eyes with the dramatic flair only pre-teens could manage. "You're embarrassing."

"Watch the eye rolls, young lady," David told her. "Everything I do is embarrassing according to Emma," David said conspiratorially to Tasha. "It's my job as a father."

Jake, who appeared to be about nine and was a perfect miniature version of Grayson, bounded up to them with a baseball glove on one hand and what looked like a well-worn trading card in the other. "Uncle Gray! Are there really cows here? Mom said there were cows."

"There are definitely cows," Grayson confirmed, ruffling his nephew's hair. "Earl's got a whole herd just down the road. Maybe we can drive by them after dinner."

"That would be awesome!" Jake turned to Tasha with the direct curiosity of childhood. "Are you really a doctor? Like, a people doctor, not an animal doctor like Uncle Gray?"

"I am," Tasha said, charmed by his earnest interest. "I work with people who are hurt or sick."

"That's so cool. Do you ever have to do surgery and stuff?"

"Jake," Caroline warned gently, "maybe save some questions for dinner?"

"It's fine," Tasha assured her, then crouched down to Jake's level. "I do sometimes help with surgery, but mostly I help people who have gotten hurt in accidents or are very sick. It's a little different from what your uncle does with animals, but we both try to help patients feel better."

"Uncle Gray recently saved a horse," Jake announced proudly. "Mom, remember I told you about Thunder?"

"You did indeed," Caroline said, her eyes finding Grayson's

with obvious affection. "It sounds like you've been keeping busy."

"Come in, come in," Grayson said, ushering everyone toward the house. "Dinner's almost ready, and it's warmer inside."

As they moved into the living room, Tasha found herself observing the family dynamics with professional interest and personal curiosity. Caroline and David moved around each other with the easy coordination of a long-married couple, while Emma helped corral Jake's boundless energy with the patience of an experienced older sister.

"Your home is beautiful," Caroline said, taking in the comfortable furnishings and the flowers Tasha had arranged that morning. "It feels so... settled. Peaceful."

"Thank you. We've been working on making it feel like home."

"We?" Emma asked, then looked between Tasha and Grayson with the shrewd perception of adolescence. "So you live here? Together?"

"Emma," David said mildly, "personal questions can wait until at least after appetizers."

"It's okay," Tasha said, feeling heat rise in her face but determined to be honest. "Yes, we live together. I moved in recently."

"That's awesome," Jake declared with the uncomplicated acceptance of childhood. "Uncle Gray seems really happy now."

"Jake's very observant," Caroline said with a meaningful look at Tasha. "He notices when people are genuinely content."

As they settled in the living room with drinks—hot cocoa with marshmallows—the conversation flowed with surprising ease. Caroline wanted to know about Tasha's work at the clinic and the hospital, while David was fascinated by their emergency response partnership.

"So you actually work together on cases?" David asked, leaning forward with academic interest. "How does that coordination work in practice?"

"It started organically," Tasha explained. "Farm accidents often involve both injured people and animals. Having both skill sets available on-site can be crucial."

"That's brilliant," Caroline said admiringly. "Rural health-care is so often fragmented. You're creating an integrated approach."

Emma, after her initial shyness wore off, peppered Tasha with questions about medical school and what it was like being one of the few women in emergency medicine.

"Do people ever not take you seriously because you're young?" Emma asked, her expression serious. "I want to be a scientist, but my friend Madison says people won't listen to me because I'm a girl."

"Sometimes," Tasha admitted honestly. "But I've learned that the best response is to be so good at what you do that they have to take you seriously. And to surround yourself with people who respect your abilities—like your uncle does."

She caught Grayson's warm look across the room and felt a flutter of happiness at how naturally this was all unfolding.

"Uncle Gray respects everyone," Jake announced loyally. "He even listens to me when I tell him about baseball cards."

"That's because you're an expert," Grayson said seriously. "And experts deserve respect regardless of their age."

When Tasha excused herself to check on dinner, Caroline followed her into the kitchen.

"Can I help with anything?" Caroline asked, but her tone suggested she had more than cooking assistance in mind.

"Just keeping me company while I check on the roast," Tasha said, opening the oven to peek at their dinner.

Caroline settled against the counter, watching Tasha move around the kitchen with obvious assessment. "You know, I have to admit I was curious about you."

Tasha's hands stilled on the oven door. "Curious how?"

"When Grayson started mentioning you in our phone calls,

there was something different in his voice. More... alive, I guess. I wanted to meet the person who'd brought that back."

"And?" Tasha asked, trying to keep her voice light.

"And I can see why he's so happy. You two have this ease together—like you've been a team for years instead of months."

Relief flooded through Tasha so quickly it made her dizzy. "He makes it easy to be myself."

"That's exactly what he needs. Someone who sees him as he really is and loves that person."

They worked together to finish dinner preparations, Caroline proving to be an efficient and unobtrusive helper. As they carried serving dishes to the dining room, Tasha found herself relaxing in a way she hadn't expected. This felt natural, comfortable—like being welcomed into something rather than being tested for worthiness.

Dinner was a lively affair. Jake dominated much of the conversation with detailed explanations of his baseball card collection, while Emma regaled them with stories from school and her ambitious plans for her science fair project. David and Grayson fell into easy conversation about everything from veterinary medicine to college basketball, and Caroline seemed content to orchestrate the controlled chaos of family dinner conversation.

"This roast is incredible," Caroline said.

"Thank you. It's actually your grandmother's recipe, though I may have added a few touches of my own."

"Well, it's delicious," Caroline added. "Grayson, you didn't tell me Tasha was such a good cook."

"I'm still discovering her talents," Grayson said, his tone warm with affection. "She's full of surprises."

"Good surprises, I hope," Emma said with the directness of youth.

"The best kind," Grayson confirmed, meeting Tasha's eyes across the table.

"The vegetables are awesome as well," David said, focusing on the vegetarian sides Tasha had prepared. "Everything is perfectly seasoned."

After dinner, they moved to the living room where Jake finally got his chance to show Grayson his latest baseball card acquisitions while Emma helped Tasha clear the dishes despite protests that she was a guest.

"I like helping," Emma explained as they loaded the dishwasher. "And besides, I wanted to ask you something without everyone listening."

"What's that?"

"Do you really love Uncle Grayson?"

The question was so direct, so matter-of-fact, that Tasha nearly dropped the plate she was holding. "That's... yes. Yes, I really do."

"Good. Because he's been different since he met you—happier. And not just pretending-to-be-happy, but really happy." Emma paused, studying Tasha's face with twelve-year-old seriousness. "I think you're perfect for him."

The simple declaration made Tasha's throat tight with emotion. "Thank you. That means more than you know."

"You don't try too hard to make us like you," Emma continued with typical pre-teen bluntness. "That's how I know you're genuine."

When they rejoined the others in the living room, Tasha found David deep in conversation with Grayson about their integrated practice model.

"It's fascinating," David was saying. "You're essentially creating a new paradigm for rural healthcare delivery."

"That's all Tasha's vision," Grayson said. "I just help with the animal side of things."

"Don't let him downplay his contributions," Tasha said, settling beside him on the couch. "The whole model only works because we complement each other's expertise."

"Like a real partnership," Caroline observed with approval.

As the evening wound toward its close, the conversation turned to future plans and possibilities. Caroline was particularly interested in their professional collaboration, while David peppered them with questions about rural life and community medicine.

"You know what strikes me most about you two?" Caroline said as they prepared to leave for the bed and breakfast. "You fit. Not just as a couple, but in this life you've built together."

"It feels like we do," Tasha agreed, surprised by her own certainty.

The goodbyes were warm and included multiple promises to stay in touch and plans for the next morning's breakfast at the bed and breakfast.

"I want you to email me," Caroline told Tasha as they hugged goodbye. "I have about a million questions about your integrated practice model that I didn't get to ask tonight."

"I'd love that," Tasha said, meaning it completely.

"And we'll see you bright and early for Rochelle's famous pancakes," Grayson added. "She's already excited about meeting you all."

"Looking forward to it," David said, shaking Grayson's hand. "Tonight was wonderful. Thank you for welcoming us into your home."

After they left, Tasha and Grayson settled on the back porch with the remainder of the cocoa, both quiet as they processed the evening.

"So," Grayson said finally, "what's the verdict?"

"They're wonderful. Warm and funny and completely genuine." She leaned against his shoulder. "Emma asked me if I really loved you."

"She did? What did you tell her?"

"The truth. That I do."

Grayson was quiet for a long moment. "How did that feel?

Being questioned by my twelve-year-old niece about our relationship?"

"Surprisingly natural. Like she was just checking to make sure I was worthy of someone she loves." Tasha turned to look at him. "I think I passed."

"You more than passed. Did you see Caroline's face when you were talking about our emergency protocols? She was practically taking notes."

"And David seemed genuinely fascinated by the integrated approach. I don't think he was just being polite."

"He wasn't. When David's academically interested in something, you can tell. He gets this focused expression and starts asking very specific questions."

They sat in comfortable silence for a while, watching the stars appear in the clear Georgia sky. Tasha found herself reflecting on how different this evening had been from her expectations. She'd been prepared for polite assessment, careful questions, the kind of formal getting-to-know-you process she'd experienced with Brandon's family.

Instead, she'd found warmth, genuine interest, and the kind of easy acceptance that made her feel like she'd always been part of their circle.

"Grayson?"

"Mmm?"

"Thank you for sharing them with me. Your family is exactly what I always hoped a family could be."

"Thank you for being exactly the kind of person they'd love. Though honestly, I knew they would."

"How could you be so sure?"

"Because they raised me to recognize good people. And you, Tasha Jenkins, are the best person I know."

As they headed inside to finish cleaning up the dinner dishes, Tasha felt a deep sense of contentment settle over her. She'd found something tonight that she hadn't even realized she'd been looking for—acceptance not just as Grayson's girlfriend, but as herself. Caroline and David and even the kids had been interested in her thoughts, her work, her dreams, not just her relationship to Grayson.

"One more thing," she said as they turned off the lights and headed upstairs.

"What's that?"

"I think I understand now why you turned out to be such a good man. Your family—they're genuinely kind people who care about substance over surface."

"They liked you too. A lot. Caroline's already planning to invite us to Nashville for Thanksgiving."

"Really?"

"Really. Welcome to the Mitchell family, Tasha. Hope you're ready for a lifetime of enthusiastic involvement in your personal business."

As they settled into bed, Tasha realized that for the first time in her adult life, the prospect of family involvement didn't feel overwhelming or intrusive. It felt like belonging.

It felt like home.

CHAPTER TWENTY

The morning after Caroline's family left for Savannah, Grayson found himself humming as he prepared for his first call of the day. The visit had gone better than he'd dared hope—watching Tasha seamlessly integrate with his family had confirmed what he'd known in his heart for months. She belonged in his life completely, in every aspect of it.

His phone rang as he was loading supplies into his truck. Dr. Martinez from the hospital.

"Dr. Mitchell? I hope I'm not calling too early."

"Not at all. What can I do for you?"

"I wanted to update you on the response to your emergency partnership protocols. We've had three more hospitals in rural Georgia contact us asking for information about implementing similar programs."

Grayson paused in his loading. "Three more?"

"The word is spreading through medical networks. Apparently, several emergency department chiefs have been discussing your integrated response model at conferences. They're calling it innovative and cost-effective."

Pride swelled in Grayson's chest, though he knew the credit belonged primarily to Tasha. "That's incredible news."

"There's more. The state medical board wants to schedule a formal review of your protocols with an eye toward recommending them as a best practice model for rural emergency services."

"When?"

"Next month. They'd send a team here to observe your coordination procedures and interview both you and Dr. Jenkins about the implementation process."

After ending the call, Grayson sat in his truck for a moment, processing the implications. What had started as a practical solution to local emergency needs was becoming something much larger—a potential model that could change how rural healthcare was delivered across the state.

His first call was to the Patterson farm, where a young colt had developed a limp overnight. As he examined the animal, Mrs. Patterson hovered nearby with the kind of maternal concern that extended to all creatures under her care.

"Will he be alright, Doc?" she asked as Grayson palpated the colt's leg.

"Just a stone bruise. Nothing serious, but he'll need a few days of rest." He applied a protective bandage and handed her a bottle of anti-inflammatory medication. "Keep him in the paddock near the barn and give him one of these twice a day."

"Thank you. I don't know what we'd do without you." She paused, studying his face with the shrewd assessment that came from years of observing people. "You seem particularly cheerful this morning. I heard your family visited yesterday."

"They did. They wanted to meet Tasha."

"And how did that go?"

"Perfectly. My sister already invited us to Nashville for Thanksgiving."

Mrs. Patterson's face lit up with genuine pleasure. "That's

wonderful news. It's so nice to see you building those connections again." She hesitated, then added, "Martha mentioned that Dr. Jenkins has been getting some recognition for your emergency partnership work."

Word traveled fast in small towns, but Grayson was continually amazed by the efficiency of the Sweetgum Meadows information network. "The state medical board is interested in our protocols."

"Well, of course they are. What you two have created makes perfect sense for communities like ours." She walked him back to his truck. "Mark my words, this is just the beginning. You and Dr. Jenkins are going to make a real difference."

His next call took him to Earl's farm, where Earl wanted him to examine a bull that had been acting sluggish. Grayson found nothing seriously wrong—just the beginning of a minor respiratory infection that would respond well to antibiotics.

"Good to catch it early," Earl said as they watched the bull amble back to join the herd. "Doc, can I ask you something?"

"Of course."

"This partnership you and Dr. Jenkins have developed—is it going to take you away from regular veterinary work?"

The question surprised Grayson. "What do you mean?"

"I mean, if you become some kind of state model for emergency medicine, are you still going to be available for regular farm calls? Because I've got to tell you, the thought of losing you to bigger things has me worried."

Grayson understood Earl's concern. Rural communities had a long history of losing good professionals to opportunities in larger cities or more prestigious positions.

"Earl, this partnership isn't about leaving Sweetgum Meadows. It's about making our services here better, more comprehensive. If anything, the recognition might bring more resources to our community."

"You sure about that?"

"I'm sure. This is my home now. Our home. We're not going anywhere."

Earl's weathered face relaxed into a smile. "Good to hear. And Doc? I'm proud of what you and Dr. Jenkins have built. It's something special."

The rest of the morning was filled with routine calls, but Grayson found himself thinking about Earl's question. Recognition from the state medical board was flattering, but it also brought responsibilities and expectations. He needed to make sure that success didn't pull them away from the community-focused practice that had brought them together.

He was driving home for lunch when his phone rang with a call from a number he didn't recognize.

"Dr. Mitchell? This is Dr. Sarah Chen from the University of Georgia College of Veterinary Medicine. I hope you have a few minutes to talk."

"Of course. What can I do for you?"

"I'm calling about your emergency response partnership with Dr. Jenkins. We've been following the development of your protocols, and frankly, we're impressed."

"Thank you. Dr. Jenkins deserves most of the credit for the conceptual framework."

"Actually, that's what makes it so interesting. The collaboration between human and veterinary medicine is exactly the kind of innovative approach we want to encourage in our students." Dr. Chen paused. "Would you and Dr. Jenkins be interested in speaking to our senior veterinary students about integrated practice models?"

Grayson found himself smiling. "I think we'd be very interested."

"Excellent. We're planning a symposium on rural veterinary practice next month. Your presentation could be a real inspiration for students who are considering careers in underserved communities."

After arranging the details, Grayson headed home with a growing sense of excitement. Teaching, sharing their model with the next generation of veterinarians—it felt like a natural evolution of their work.

He found Tasha in their makeshift office, surrounded by medical journals and looking more animated than he'd seen her in weeks.

"Good morning?" he asked, noting the scattered papers and the barely touched cup of coffee beside her.

"The best morning," she said, looking up with sparkling eyes. "I just got off the phone with Dr. Rodriguez from the State Medical Association. They want to feature our integrated practice model in their quarterly journal."

"That's fantastic."

"It gets better. They also want to recommend us for the Rural Healthcare Innovation Award. It comes with a grant that could fund equipment and training for other communities interested in implementing similar programs."

Grayson settled into the chair beside her, taking in the scope of materials she'd spread across the desk. "This is really happening, isn't it? Our little emergency partnership is becoming something bigger."

"Much bigger. And I just realized something." She turned to face him fully. "A few months ago, the idea of this kind of professional recognition would have terrified me. I would have been convinced I didn't deserve it, that someone would discover I was a fraud."

"And now?"

"Now I know we've earned this. We've built something innovative and effective that genuinely helps people. I'm proud of what we've accomplished."

The confidence in her voice made Grayson's chest warm with affection and admiration. This was the woman he'd always seen in her—brilliant, capable, deserving of every accolade and opportunity.

"Speaking of accomplishments," he said, "I got a call from U-G-A's vet school. They want us to speak at a symposium on rural practice."

"Really? That's wonderful. When?"

"Next month. And Dr. Martinez called this morning—three more hospitals want information about our protocols, and the state medical board wants to do a formal review."

Tasha leaned back in her chair, a slightly overwhelmed expression crossing her face. "It's all happening so fast."

"Too fast?"

"No, not too fast. Just... unexpected. I came here thinking I was retreating from my career, and instead I've found something more meaningful than anything I ever did in Atlanta."

They spent the next hour discussing the various opportunities and commitments that were suddenly appearing. Speaking engagements, journal articles, site visits from other medical professionals—their quiet life in Sweetgum Meadows was about to become much busier.

"Are you worried about the attention?" Tasha asked as they prepared lunch together.

"A little," Grayson admitted. "Earl asked this morning if all this recognition might take me away from regular practice. I assured him it wouldn't, but I want to make sure that's true."

"It will be. The whole point of our model is that it serves local communities better. If we let success pull us away from that foundation, we'd be undermining everything we've built."

"Agreed. But we'll need to be intentional about maintaining that balance."

Their conversation was interrupted by a knock at the front door. Grayson opened it to find Aria standing on their porch, her expression excited but slightly nervous.

"Dr. Mitchell? I hope I'm not bothering you, but I wanted to ask you something."

"Of course, Aria. What's on your mind?"

"Well, you know how I've been learning about veterinary medicine? And how I helped with Thunder and the other emergencies?"

"You've been doing excellent work."

"Thank you. But I was wondering..." She took a deep breath, gathering her courage. "Would it be okay if I kept helping you sometimes? Like, when I'm not in school? I really want to learn as much as I can, and Mom says it's okay as long as you don't mind having me around."

Grayson exchanged a look with Tasha, who had joined them at the door. He'd been impressed by Aria's growing confidence and competence around animals, and her enthusiasm for learning was infectious.

"What kind of helping did you have in mind?"

"Just watching and learning, mostly. Maybe helping with simple things when you think I'm ready. I know I'm too young for real work, but I want to understand as much as possible about taking care of animals."

"And your mom's really okay with this?"

"She said she's proud of how much I've learned already. She thinks it's good for me to have something I'm passionate about."

Grayson felt a deep satisfaction at her conviction. "In that case, yes. I'd be happy to have you continue helping when you can. We'll make sure it doesn't interfere with school, and you'll stick to observation and simple tasks."

Aria's face lit up with pure joy. "Really? Thank you so much, Dr. Mitchell. I promise I won't get in the way, and I'll listen to everything you teach me."

After she left, practically skipping with excitement, Tasha smiled at Grayson. "You realize what you just did?"

"What?"

"You just inspired the next generation. That little girl is going to grow up knowing she can do anything she sets her mind to."

The observation struck him as profoundly true. Their practice was growing not just in scope and recognition, but in its impact on the next generation. Aria would probably go on to veterinary school with real experience and confidence, hopefully carrying forward the integrated approach they'd pioneered.

"It feels right," he said finally. "Like everything else we've built here—it feels like the natural next step."

That evening, as they worked together to prepare materials for their upcoming speaking engagement, Grayson reflected on how much their lives had changed in just a few months. What had started as a personal relationship had evolved into a professional partnership that was gaining recognition far beyond their small community.

"This is surreal," Tasha said as she reviewed their presentation outline. "Six months ago, I was hiding from my career. Now we're being asked to teach other professionals."

"It's well-deserved recognition for innovative work."

"It's validation that we chose the right path. That building something together was worth the risk."

Grayson watched her as she organized their materials, noting the confidence in her movements, the excitement in her voice when she talked about their future projects. This was the woman he'd fallen in love with—brilliant, passionate, completely in her element when working toward something meaningful.

"What are you thinking about?" she asked, catching him staring.

"Just... this. Us. How perfectly everything has fallen into place."

"It has, hasn't it? Sometimes I can hardly believe this is my life now."

As they finished their work and prepared for bed, Grayson found himself thinking about the future with a clarity that surprised him. All the professional success, all the recognition and opportunities—they were wonderful, but they weren't the most important thing.

The most important thing was the woman beside him, and the life they were building together. And lately, he'd been thinking more and more about making that partnership official in every possible way.

Soon, he decided. Very soon.

CHAPTER TWENTY-ONE

Three weeks had passed since their speaking engagement at U-G-A, and Grayson had been carrying the ring in his truck's glove compartment for the last ten days. Every time he thought he'd found the perfect moment to propose, something had interrupted—an emergency call, a speaking engagement, visits from medical professionals wanting to observe their protocols.

The ring itself had been surprisingly easy to choose. He'd driven to Atlanta on the pretext of picking up specialized equipment, but really to visit the jeweler Patricia Williams had recommended when she'd called to congratulate them on their professional recognition. A simple solitaire that caught the light beautifully, classic enough to suit Tasha's understated elegance but with a vintage setting that spoke to the timeless nature of what they were building together.

Now, as he finished his morning calls, Grayson found himself more nervous than he'd been since his first day of veterinary school. He'd planned the proposal carefully—tonight, after dinner, at the place where they'd first worked together saving Stormy during the storm. Earl had already agreed to make sure the barn was prepared, and Tasha thought they were just stopping by to check on a horse that had been showing signs of mild colic.

His phone buzzed with a text from Caroline: "How's the proposal planning going? Do you need moral support?"

He'd made the mistake of telling his sister about his intentions during their last phone call, and she'd been offering advice and encouragement ever since. The family ring discussion had been particularly intense, with Caroline advocating for their grandmother's antique setting while their mother insisted on something more modern. In the end, he'd chosen something that felt right for Tasha specifically.

"Tonight's the night," he texted back. "Wish me luck."

"You don't need luck. You need courage. Which you have. She's going to say yes, Gray. I saw how she looked at you when we visited."

The vote of confidence helped settle his nerves as he drove home for lunch. Tasha was in the kitchen, reviewing patient charts while eating a sandwich, looking perfectly content with their domestic routine.

"How was your morning?" she asked, looking up with the smile that never failed to make his chest warm.

"Good. Routine calls, nothing dramatic. How about you?"

"Busy. Dr. Martinez wants me to review the protocols for that journal article one more time, and I'm supposed to call Dr. Chen about scheduling more speaking engagements." She paused, studying his face. "You seem... I don't know. Distracted?"

Grayson felt his skin flush. "Just thinking about tonight's check on Earl's horse."

"Is there something concerning about that situation?"

"No, nothing concerning. Just... important."

If Tasha found his answer odd, she didn't press. Instead, she returned to her charts while he made himself lunch, trying to act normal despite the ring burning a hole in his jacket pocket.

The afternoon dragged interminably. Every patient seemed to require extended consultation, every call ran longer than expected, and by the time he finished his last appointment, Grayson was running behind schedule. He'd planned to pick up flowers and stop by the house to change clothes, but instead he found himself racing home just in time for their dinner plans.

"Ready to go check on that horse?" Tasha asked as he hurried through the door.

"Actually, I thought we could eat first. I made reservations at that little place in the next town over."

"Reservations?" Tasha raised an eyebrow. "Since when do you make dinner reservations for a routine farm call?"

"Since I thought it might be nice to have a proper date night. We've been so busy with work lately."

The explanation seemed to satisfy her, though Grayson caught her giving him curious looks throughout dinner. The restaurant was perfect—quiet enough for conversation, romantic enough to set the right mood, but not so formal as to seem out of character for their usual habits.

"This is lovely," Tasha said over dessert. "What's the occasion?"

"Do I need an occasion to take my girlfriend to a nice dinner?"

"Girlfriend," she repeated with amusement. "Such a inadequate word for what we are, don't you think?"

The opening was perfect, but Grayson felt his prepared speech evaporate. "What would you call us?"

"Partners. In every sense of the word." She reached across the table to take his hand. "I love what we've built together, Grayson. Professionally, personally, all of it."

"Even when it gets chaotic? When we're being pulled in different directions by speaking engagements and site visits?"

"Especially then. Because we're handling it together, as a team. That's what makes it work."

By the time they finished dinner, the sun was setting, painting the sky in shades of pink and gold that seemed designed for romantic gestures. Grayson's nervousness had transformed into something more like anticipation as they drove toward Earl's farm.

"It's beautiful tonight," Tasha observed, watching the countryside pass by in the gathering dusk.

"Perfect weather for being outside."

"Good thing, since we'll be in a barn."

Earl was waiting for them when they arrived, his expression carefully neutral despite the significance of the evening. "Evening, Doc, Dr. Jenkins. The horse is in the main barn, same stall as usual."

Grayson had asked Earl to make sure the barn was clean and well-lit, with fresh hay and flowers—simple touches that would create the right atmosphere without seeming too obviously planned. As they walked toward the building, he caught sight of Earl's handiwork and felt a surge of gratitude for his friend's attention to detail.

"It smells different in here," Tasha commented as they entered the barn. "Like flowers."

"Earl's been experimenting with natural air fresheners," Grayson improvised, leading her toward the stall where they'd first worked together during the storm months ago.

The stall was empty of animals but filled with soft light from battery-powered lanterns Earl had strategically placed. Fresh wildflowers from the fields surrounding the farm had been arranged in simple mason jars, and clean hay covered the floor like a golden carpet.

"Grayson," Tasha said slowly, "there's no sick horse here."

"No," he agreed, his heart hammering against his ribs. "There isn't."

She turned to face him fully, her expression shifting from

confusion to something that looked like understanding. "What's going on?"

Instead of answering with words, Grayson pulled the ring box from his jacket pocket and dropped to one knee in the place where they'd first discovered how perfectly they worked together.

"Tasha Jenkins," he began, his voice steadier than he'd expected, "You walked into my life during a storm and you've been making everything brighter ever since."

Her hands flew to cover her mouth, tears already shining in her eyes.

"I brought you here because this is where I first saw who you really are. Not the broken woman hiding from her past, but the brilliant, compassionate, brave person who jumped in to help save a calf's life without hesitation." He opened the ring box, revealing the diamond that caught the lantern light and threw it back in sparkles across the barn walls. "This is where I fell in love with you, and this is where I want to promise you forever."

"Grayson," she whispered through her tears.

"I love your dedication to healing people. I love the way you argue with medical journals when they publish studies you disagree with. I love that you chose to build a life here, with me, even when it meant leaving everything familiar behind."

He took a shaky breath, the prepared words giving way to what was in his heart.

"I love that we're better together than either of us ever was alone. I want to marry you, Tasha. I want to build a practice and a family and a lifetime with you. Will you marry me?"

For a moment that felt like eternity, she stared at him through her tears. Then she dropped to her knees in the hay beside him, framing his face with trembling hands.

"Yes," she said, her voice breaking with emotion. "Yes, of course, yes."

The ring slid onto her finger perfectly, as if it had been made for her hand specifically. When Grayson kissed her, there in the soft light of the barn where they'd first become partners, it felt like coming full circle and starting fresh all at the same time.

"I can't believe you did this here," she said when they broke apart, both of them laughing and crying. "It's perfect."

"I wanted it to be somewhere that mattered to us. Somewhere that represented what we've built together."

"Emergency veterinary medicine in a storm?"

"Partnership. Trust. The willingness to jump in and help even when you're scared."

She kissed him again, softer this time, full of promise. "I love you so much. I love the life we've created, and I love that we're going to make it official."

From outside the barn came the sound of applause. They looked up to see Earl standing in the doorway, grinning widely.

"About time," he called out. "Congratulations, both of you."

"Earl!" Tasha laughed, wiping at her tears. "How long have you been standing there?"

"Long enough to make sure he didn't mess it up. Though I have to say, Doc, that was pretty smooth for a veterinarian."

"Thanks for your help with all this," Grayson said, standing and pulling Tasha up with him.

"My pleasure. You two are good for each other, and this community's better for having you both." Earl's expression grew serious. "Leslie would have been happy for you, Doc. She always wanted you to find love again."

The mention of Leslie's name might have felt awkward months ago, but now it just felt like a blessing from someone who had loved Grayson enough to want his future happiness.

"Thank you," Grayson said quietly. "That means a lot."

As they walked back to the truck, Tasha kept looking down at her ring, the diamond catching the last light of sunset.

"When did you get this? How long have you been planning this?"

"I bought it two weeks ago. I've been planning it since my family visited and I saw how perfectly you fit into every part of my life."

"Caroline knew, didn't she? She kept asking me pointed questions about commitment and future plans."

"I may have mentioned my intentions during our last phone call."

"And she didn't give anything away. I'm impressed by her restraint."

They drove home through the gathering darkness, hands linked across the center console, Tasha's engagement ring sparkling every time they passed under a streetlight. The practical details of wedding planning lay ahead—dates and venues and guest lists—but for now, Grayson was content to simply absorb the reality that she'd said yes.

"Should we call people?" Tasha asked as they pulled into their driveway. "Tell them the news?"

"Who do you want to call first?"

"Your family. They're going to be so excited."

"Actually," Grayson said, remembering Caroline's text from that morning, "I think they're already expecting this call."

Inside, they settled on the couch with wine and Grayson's phone, calling Caroline first, then his parents, then working through their list of friends and colleagues who had become family. Each conversation brought fresh congratulations and excitement, each person adding their voice to the chorus of support that had surrounded their relationship from the beginning.

"The book club is going to lose their minds," Tasha said after calling Brandi, who had immediately put her on speaker so the other women could shriek their congratulations. "Mrs. Bridges said she's already planning the engagement party."

"Of course she is."

"Are you ready for that? For the whole community to be involved in our wedding planning?"

Grayson considered the question seriously. Several months ago, the idea of community involvement in his personal life would have felt overwhelming. Now it just felt like being surrounded by people who cared about their happiness.

"I think I am. Are you?"

"More than ready. I want everyone to be part of this—your family, our friends, the whole town if they want to be." She curled against his side, her ring catching the lamplight. "I want this to be a celebration of not just us, but of the life we've built here together."

As they talked late into the night about their hopes for their wedding and their future, Grayson felt a deep sense of completion. The ring on Tasha's finger was just a symbol, but what it represented—their commitment to building a life together, their willingness to take the leap into forever—felt like the most natural thing in the world.

"Grayson?"

"Mmm?"

"Thank you for choosing the perfect place to propose. And for choosing me."

"Thank you for saying yes. And for choosing this life with me."

Outside, Sweetgum Meadows settled into peaceful sleep around them, the community that had become their home already preparing to celebrate their next chapter. And inside, two people who had found healing and love and purpose in each other's arms planned for a future that promised to be everything they'd ever dreamed of and more.

EPILOGUE

SIX MONTHS LATER...

The morning sun streamed through the windows of Sweetgum Meadows Community Church, casting golden light across the pews that were already filling with familiar faces. Tasha stood in the small preparation room behind the sanctuary, surrounded by the women who had become her chosen family—Caroline adjusting the delicate lace sleeves of her dress, Brandi fussing with her hair, Mrs. Bridges offering last-minute wisdom, and India taking what seemed like hundreds of photos.

"You look absolutely radiant," Caroline said, stepping back to admire her handiwork. "My brother is going to cry when he sees you."

"He better not, because then I will, too," Tasha laughed, checking her reflection in the antique mirror Earl had brought from his grandmother's collection. "I spent too much time on my makeup to have him ruin it with tears."

"Oh honey," Mrs. Bridges said with the knowing smile of someone who'd attended dozens of Sweetgum Meadows weddings, "there isn't a dry eye in that sanctuary. Half the town is already weeping, and the ceremony hasn't even started."

Through the window, Tasha could see the courtyard where they'd decided to hold the reception. White lights were strung between the old oak trees, and tables covered in cream-colored linens were scattered across the grass. Malakai and Aimee of Rochelle's Old-Fashioned Diner had insisted on catering, turning the event into a true community celebration with all of Grayson's favorite dishes and several vegetarian options for the out-of-town guests.

"Are you nervous?" Caroline asked, noting Tasha's quiet contemplation.

"Not nervous," Tasha said, surprising herself with the truth of it. "Excited. Ready. This feels like the most natural thing in the world."

A year ago, she would never have imagined herself here—surrounded by women who loved her, preparing to marry a man who saw her completely and chose her anyway, in a community that had embraced her as one of their own. The journey from the broken woman who'd fled Atlanta to the confident bride adjusting her pearl earrings felt both impossibly long and remarkably quick.

"Time to go," Brandi announced as the opening notes of the processional music drifted through the door.

Tasha's heart began to race, but not with anxiety—with pure anticipation. In a few minutes, she would walk down that aisle toward the man who had taught her to trust again, to love again, to believe that broken things could be made whole.

The processional began with Aria, who had insisted on being their flower girl. She walked down the aisle with the serious concentration she brought to everything, scattering rose petals with the precision of someone who understood the importance of the moment. Emma followed as junior bridesmaid, sophisti-cated in her pale blue dress and carrying herself with the poise of someone much older.

Caroline squeezed Tasha's hand before taking her place as

matron of honor. "See you at the altar," she whispered, then walked through the door with her bouquet of white roses and baby's breath.

"Ready, my dear?" Dr. Leighton asked, appearing at her side. When Tasha had mentioned that no family would be attending, Dr. Leighton had quietly offered to walk her down the aisle, an offer that had brought her to tears and made her feel truly welcomed into the community family.

"More than ready," she said, taking his offered arm.

The music swelled, and the congregation rose as they appeared in the doorway. Tasha's breath caught at the sight before her—the church was packed with every person who mattered to them. Grayson's parents in the front row, beaming with pride. Earl and Casey and Aria's whole family. The entire book club. Dr. Martinez and the hospital staff. Patients who had become friends. Colleagues from their speaking engagements. What seemed like half of Sweetgum Meadows, all gathered to celebrate their love.

But her eyes went immediately to Grayson, standing at the altar in his navy suit, his face radiant with joy and love. The sight of him made her chest tight with emotion. This was the man who had believed in her when she couldn't believe in herself, who had shown her what true partnership meant, who had given her a home and a purpose and a love deeper than anything she'd ever imagined.

As they walked down the aisle, Tasha felt the love and support of their community surrounding them. Mrs. Patterson dabbed at her eyes with a handkerchief. Tom Bradley gave her an encouraging nod. Rashad and India beamed from their pew. The book club looked like they might burst with excitement.

"You look beautiful, my dear," Dr. Leighton whispered as they approached the altar. "And you're making the right choice."

"I know," she whispered back, her eyes never leaving Grayson's face.

When Dr. Leighton placed her hand in Grayson's, the connection between them felt electric, complete, like a circuit finally closing. His thumb traced across her knuckles, and she saw her own joy reflected in his eyes.

"Dearly beloved," Pastor Williams began, his voice warm with affection for the couple he'd watched fall in love, "we are gathered here today to witness the marriage of Grayson and Tasha, two people who have shown us all what it means to find healing and purpose in love."

The ceremony flowed around her like a dream, but Tasha felt grounded in every moment—the warmth of Grayson's hands holding hers, the faces of their friends and family beaming at them from the pews, the golden light streaming through the stained glass windows. When Pastor Williams spoke about love as a choice made daily, about partnership as a commitment to grow together, Tasha felt the truth of those words settle into her bones.

When it came time for vows, Grayson spoke first, his voice steady despite the emotion she could see threatening to overwhelm him.

"Tasha," he began, "you came into my life during a storm, and you've been my sunshine ever since. You've shown me that love isn't about replacing what was lost, but about building something new and beautiful from what remains. You're my partner in everything—in work, in life, in all the adventures still to come. I promise to support your dreams, to share your burdens, to celebrate your victories, and to love you with everything I have for the rest of our lives."

Tasha felt tears sliding down her cheeks, but she didn't care about her makeup anymore. When it was her turn to speak, the words came from her heart without hesitation.

"Grayson, you taught me that I could trust again—trust myself, trust love, trust that I deserved happiness. You've given me a home, a family, a purpose I never knew I was looking for.

You've shown me that broken things can be healed, that endings can become beginnings, that two people can build something together that's stronger than either could create alone. I promise to be your partner in all things, to love you in your strength and support you in your struggles, and to choose you, every day, for the rest of our lives."

The exchange of rings was accompanied by more tears from the congregation—Tasha caught sight of Earl wiping his eyes and Mrs. Bridges dabbing at hers with a lace handkerchief. When Pastor Williams finally pronounced them husband and wife, the church erupted in cheers that could probably be heard three counties over.

"You may kiss your bride," Pastor Williams said with a grin, but Grayson was already stepping forward, cupping her face in his hands and kissing her with all the love and joy and promise of forever that filled his heart.

The walk back down the aisle as husband and wife felt like floating. Everyone was on their feet, applauding and cheering, throwing rice and flower petals. Tasha caught glimpses of beaming faces—Caroline crying happy tears, Jake jumping up and down with excitement, the book club looking like they'd just witnessed the best romance novel ending ever written.

Outside the church, they were swept into a whirlwind of congratulations and photographs. Everyone wanted to hug them, to share their joy, to be part of this moment. Malakai appeared with glasses of champagne, grinning widely as he toasted their happiness.

"You two clean up nice," he said, raising his glass. "Now get over to that reception before Aimee starts worrying that all her food is getting cold."

The reception was everything they'd dreamed of—tables full of Malakai's incredible cooking, dancing under the stars, toasts that ranged from hilarious to deeply moving. Earl's speech about watching two broken hearts heal each other brought everyone to tears. Caroline's toast about finding family in unexpected places had the whole crowd raising their glasses. Mrs. Bridges' blessing over their marriage felt like an official welcome into the community's heart.

As the evening wound down and guests began to filter home, Tasha found herself swaying in Grayson's arms to the last song of the night, surrounded by the remnants of their perfect celebration.

"How does it feel?" Grayson asked softly. "Being Mrs. Mitchell?"

"Perfect," she said without hesitation. "Like everything in my life finally makes sense."

"Any regrets about the small-town wedding instead of something bigger?"

Tasha looked around at the scene of their celebration—tables where their friends and neighbors had celebrated with them, the church where they'd promised forever, the community that had embraced them both.

"Are you kidding? This was perfect. This is us—surrounded by people who love us, in the place we've built our life together." She stood on her toes to kiss him softly. "Besides, where else could we have gotten away with having a reception where the main topic of conversation was livestock breeding techniques and the latest developments in rural emergency medicine?"

"Nowhere," Grayson agreed, laughing. "Only in Sweetgum Meadows would that be considered romantic wedding conversation."

As they walked toward his truck—now decorated with tin cans and ribbons courtesy of Jake and his friends—Tasha paused to look back at the scene of their celebration. The lights were still twinkling in the trees, and a few stragglers were helping clean up, but the magical evening was coming to an end.

"Thank you," she said quietly.

"For what?"

"For showing me what home really means. For giving me a family. For proving that sometimes the best things come after the worst things."

"Thank you for being brave enough to start over. For choosing this life, this town, me."

"Best decision I ever made."

They drove through the quiet streets of Sweetgum Meadows toward the house they'd shared for months but that now felt different somehow—not just the place they lived, but the foundation of their married life. Tomorrow they would leave for their honeymoon, a week at a cabin in the mountains where they could disconnect from veterinary emergencies and medical conferences and just be newlyweds.

But tonight, they were home in every sense of the word—in their community, in their love, in the life they'd built together from two broken hearts and the courage to try again.

"I love you, Mrs. Mitchell," Grayson said as they pulled into their driveway.

"I love you too, Mr. Mitchell," she replied, her wedding ring catching the porch light as she reached for his hand. "Forever and always."

And as they walked into their house together, still in their wedding clothes and giddy with joy, Tasha knew that this was just the beginning of the greatest adventure of their lives. She'd found her place in the world, her purpose, her person. She'd found home. They'd found home. Together.

Thank you so much for reading Healing Hearts, the thirteenth book in the Sweetgum Meadows Romance series of stand-alone novels. I really hope you loved it! If you enjoyed this book, please consider leaving a review so that others may also find it. Also, if you haven't read the first books yet, check them out today! Although these are stand-alone novels, the stories all intertwine and progress.

I look forward to introducing you to the other characters in this lovely, family-oriented town where each couple will find their happily ever after.

You can get the next books in the series by visiting ImaniPrice.com.

ALSO BY IMANI PRICE

Book 1: Love Between Us

Book 2: Sweet Sunsets

Book 3: Infinite Kiss

Book 4: Dance With Me

Book 5: In Charge

Book 6: Forever With You

Book 7: Secret Sweethearts

Book 8: Endless Love

Book 9: The Harder We Fall

Book 10: Reservations of the Heart

Book 11: Play by Play

Book 12: Guarded Hearts

Book 13: Healing Hearts

Book 14: Dear Sweetgum

Book 15: Lanterns of the Meadows (novella)

Book 16: Drawn to You

Book 17: Under the Sweetgum Tree

Sweetgum Meadows' Visitor's Guide

My full audiobook catalog is available for FREE on YouTube. Check
it out here: https://swiy.co/Sweetgum

To all my lovely readers,

Thank you
for
reading